Tales of Leight
Book One

Wizard Rising

By Evan Kelling

Troubled Youth

This story follows Jacob and gives us a peek at what his life is like when he's not acting as Tobias' bodyguard. The events take place concurrently with *Fang Wars*, so I'd advise you to read that story first before this one.

Chapter 1

My name is Jacob Lewis. I'm a golem in service of the Mystic Order. To many, I look no older than eighteen, but that's far from the truth. I'm actually closer to forty if I remember correctly. That was young for golem standards, though, since most of my kind was created in the 1940's.

For the better part of eighteen years, I'd been tasked with protecting a young wizard, Tobias Leight, until he discovered what he was and his training could begin. Together, we'd managed to thwart a fallen angel's plan to possess him and begin a quest for world domination. But now that his training had begun, my assignment to be his protector had come to an end. That meant that the Mystic Order could send me on other assignments. Thus, my current situation.

I was in Golden, Colorado, seated in a café across from the local youth center. I sipped on a cup of warm green tea and scrolled through my phone. Nothing on Reddit caught my attention, but I wasn't focused on it anyway. My attention was on the youth center.

Youth centers were a hot spot for troubled kids, a good percentage of them ended up being young wizards. It was a good place to scout for young talent before they got into too much trouble and grew up in warlocks. Even with the combined efforts of all the "talent scouts" in the Mystic Order, many kids still fell through the cracks. Some didn't even realize the power they possessed, even fewer actually understood what was happening to them. All they knew was that they could do things. And power like that was very easy to misuse.

But that wasn't why I was here. There'd been over a dozen reported disappearances over the last couple of weeks. All of them were kids and teens. All of them had visited this youth center, at least once. I swiped my thumb across my screen and switched to my photo app, where I'd downloaded copies of the Mystic Orders reports of the kids. Pretty much every single one of them had some sort of record of delinquent activity.

I frowned. It wasn't fair what was happening to these kids. Many of these kids who had a talent for magic were born to mortal parents who had no idea how to handle a normal teenager, let alone one who suddenly developed abilities. And now on top of it all, they were going missing. It had become such an issue that the Mystic Order couldn't help but take notice.

For a supernatural predator, the youth center was an ideal hunting ground. The kids had it rough and just wanted someone to see them, to accept them. It made them impressionable and easy to coerce. It made them easy prey. I'd seen it in plenty of old Mystic Order case files.

I'd been scoping out this place for a couple of days now with little success. I sipped on my tea and returned to Reddit, keeping one eye on the youth center. After another twenty minutes of doom scrolling, something finally caught my attention. There was a scrawny kid with an oversized backpack approaching the building. He was twelve years old, maybe thirteen and looked like he desperately needed a trip to a professional barber. His messy black hair was cut unevenly in places and made him look more disheveled than he actually was.

But it wasn't him that concerned me. It was the group of three older boys coming up behind him that set off alarm bells. There were two tall, gangly teens that could've been twins, both with long brown hair styled into mullets. One wore a bright red shirt and his twin wore a navy blue shirt. The boy between them was a bit shorter, but taller than the disheveled kid I'd first seen. What he lacked in height, he made up for in pudginess, made all the more evident by his gray t-shirt that was a couple sizes too small. They'd stalked him like wolves to a doe up the stairs leading to the youth center. Navy shirt made the first move, slinking up behind the disheveled kid and forcefully yanking his backpack away. I couldn't hear them from this distance but I saw the surprise and alarm on disheveled kid's face as he turned to face his attackers. Navy shirt slung the backpack over his shoulder as his twin in red pushed the disheveled kid down to the ground. I saw the trio's shoulders rise and fall as they laughed. Pudgy kid made a follow-me motion and the three kids took off.

I recognized a look of dismay on disheveled kid's face, but I didn't get up. Not yet. The kid picked himself up and pursued the trio, I assumed in hopes of getting his backpack back. He started moving, his movements stiff. His fall had probably caused some soreness or scrapes that he was now nursing. The bully trio hurried down the stairs and made a couple turns, disappearing down an alley. The poor kid they'd stolen from following a fair distance behind.

I debated pursuing them. After all, this could just be a scuffle between some regular mortal kids. But a bad feeling tickled at the back of my mind. I decided to follow them. After all, there was no reason I couldn't help the kid out, even if he was just a regular kid. It just meant I'd have to keep a lid on my supernatural abilities.

Being a golem granted me a plethora of supernatural abilities. It made me stronger and more durable and gave me access to a limited pool of spells and magic. Perfect for smashing demons and ghouls, but probably inappropriate to use in a conflict with a few punk teenagers.

I downed the remaining half of my tea and pocketed my phone, swiftly exiting the café and moving purposely to where I'd last seen the four boys. The alley they'd gone down kept them hidden from prying eyes. It'd be the perfect place for a fledgling wizard to test their abilities on an unsuspecting victim.

I jabbed the crosswalk button and waited patiently for the light to change. After several aggravating seconds, the light changed and I hurried across the street, my eyes locked on the alleyway where the boys had disappeared. Once across the street, I sped past the youth center, spun on my heel, and headed down the alley. The trio of boys had managed to corner the disheveled kid at the end of the alley. Navy, Red, and Pudgy all took turns taunting and pushing the kid.

I stopped, frowning. They hadn't noticed me yet. I decided to wait a moment and see what they would do.

"Come on freak, show us your tricks!" Navy jabbed, pushing the kid hard on the shoulder.

"You're probably just full of shit!" Red added, pushing the poor kid back towards Navy.

"Stop! Give it back!" Disheveled kid pleaded. He lunged forward awkwardly; his balance was poor. He probably had no experience in fighting.

Pudgy intercepted the boy, blocking him from reaching Navy and his backpack. He pushed the boy hard enough that he hit the wall, his head rocking back and making an ugly thudding sound against the wall.

"You're always telling us about your cool powers or whatever, but I know you're just full of shit!" Pudgy boy sneered.

I perked up at that. Powers?

Disheveled kid gritted his teeth, a look of renewed determination taking over his expression. "Oh yeah? I'll show you!" The boy took a policeman's firing stance, holding his fingers out in the shape of a gun.

The bully trio burst out laughing. Pudgy doubled over in hysterics as they continued to taunt him. But my attention was focused on the disheveled kid. That's when I felt it. The surge of magical energies gathering.

It was sloppy, but the kid was definitely gathering magic in.

Finally he shouted. *"Bang bang!"*

There was a surge of motion in the air and an invisible force struck Pudgy kid right as he stood up straight. Pudgy was flung through the air, flying back four feet or so. Navy and Red looked at their fallen leader in disbelief. They were so shocked they still had yet to notice me. Disheveled kid might have, but that spell must've taken a lot out of him, because his eyes rolled back for a brief second and he slumped to his knees on the ground.

Navy and Red's expressions turned from surprise to frightened anger. They turned back to the boy and started kicking him. Disheveled kid let out a pained cry and fell to a prone position, and his attackers weren't letting up.

"You fucking freak!" Navy growled.

"How'd you even do that?" Red added.

The poor kid couldn't get a word in edgewise in between the blows. So I decided it was time to finally step in. I hurried down the length of the alley, passing the pudgy kid without a second thought. I hated bullies. I had to put up with them for all my life, due to my less than stellar looks. I'd never been able to fight back, in fear of hurting them or otherwise revealing my true nature. But Tobias had always stepped in on my behalf, even when it was a losing battle. It's one of the many reasons I'd realized that when it came down to it, our friendship was more than just a job to me.

I closed the distance between me and the two remaining bullies, who couldn't be bothered to notice me while they were beating on the kid. Navy was about to throw a punch when I thrust my hand out and caught it before he could begin the downward strike.

Navy turned to me, clearly shocked that he'd been discovered. With only an ounce of golem strength in play, I stepped back and hurled him towards his companion. My aim was good and Navy fell on Pudgy, his head bouncing off his friend's rotund form.

Red turned to face me next. "What the hell?"

Before he could say anything else, I planted one of my feet inside his poor stance, grabbed him by the arm and threw him over my shoulder. I guided the throw the entire way, making sure to keep his head from hitting the concrete.

The three bullies sat up to look at me as I stood between them and their chosen victim. I walked past Red, glaring at him so he'd get the message to stay down. I sauntered over to where Navy sat on the ground, still stunned from the throw and ripped the backpack from his grip.

I turned so all three of the bullies could see me address them. "Go home," I growled. "And don't let me catch you picking on this poor kid again."

They nodded, all of them sharing a dumbfounded expression. They probably weren't used to anyone standing up to them, let alone an adult who seemed to actually give a damn. None of them moved.

"Go home," I repeated myself. "Now!"

That snapped them out of their daze. Navy and Red scrambled to their feet and scurried away. Pudgy followed suit, except he tripped and fell flat on his face, before rising again and following his goons.

I walked over to where the kid had fallen, offering my hand. He shook off his daze and accepted my hand. I hauled him up and took inventory over him. He had a few scrapes and bruises, but I didn't notice anything too serious. I held out his backpack with one hand, despite its weight.

"You alright, kid?" I asked.

"Yeah. Thanks, mister." He accepted the backpack, its weight nearly toppling him over. He swung it over his shoulder and stuck his other arm through.

"What's your name, kid?" I asked.

"Uh, Jeremy." He said, his voice still a little shaky.

"Nice to meet you, Jeremy. I'm Jacob," I said. "Hell of a trick you pulled there."

Jeremy suddenly got very nervous, his eyes widening as he tried to think up an excuse or explanation.

I held up a placating hand. "Don't worry, I'm not going to tell anyone. But you should probably keep it to yourself, until you're older."

Jeremy frowned, confused by my words. "But—"

"Trust me. In time, you'll learn to control it." I said. "When you're older, there will be people who can help you learn about your abilities. But right now, it's better that you don't go showing it off. Especially to bullies like those guys. People are scared of what they don't understand."

"I guess so," Jeremy said, his voice small.

"Why don't you run along now?" I suggested. "Better to get home before those guys decide they want another piece of you."

"But, mister," Jeremy began.

"Jacob." I insisted.

"Oh, sorry. But mister Jacob, I've got questions!" Jeremy said eagerly, his eyes beaming.

I smiled, of course the kid had questions.

"Alright then, how about we get some froyo, and I'll answer whatever questions I can." I said.

I seriously doubted the bully trio were behind the strange disappearances. They hadn't given me "deadly supernatural predator" vibe. But they were still a predator I was happy to dissuade. Nevertheless, I still had a mysterious kidnapper to find. Which meant my work here wasn't done yet. The kid and I would get some frozen yogurt, and then my work would begin anew tomorrow.

"So you're sure there's no wizard school I get to go to in Britain?" Jeremy asked after having freshly polished off his large cup of frozen yogurt.

I stared at him, my mouth hanging open in shock. "We sat down five minutes ago, how did you finish all of that so fast?"

The kid had filled his cup past the brim with the frozen treat, and that wasn't even taking the metric ton of toppings he'd put on top.

"What about a camp?" Jeremy continued, as if I'd said nothing.

"Uh nope. No school, no camp." I said. "Not even a weekend seminar. Young apprentices are taught by more experienced wizards, but there are a lot more young budding wizards than there are older master wizards to teach them. Which is how we end up with rogue wizards like warlocks and sorcerers."

"What's the difference between a warlock and a sorcerer?"

I gave it some thought, reviewing my mental notes to distinguish the differences between the two. "Warlocks are independent, falling into the habits of dark magic all on their own. Sorcerers end up under the influence of an outside force, like a demon. But it's really splitting hairs so we usually just call them all warlocks."

"Demons are real?" Jeremy gasped loudly. His outburst earned us a few stares from the other patrons.

"Keep it down, kid," I urged him. "Yes, but they're usually not an issue. It takes a lot of work to summon a demon. More work than they're worth usually."

"What about blink dogs? Displacer beasts? Jabberwockies? Elves? Satyrs? Owlbears?"

It took me a minute, but I realized he was listing off creatures from Dungeons and Dragons. "No, no, not sure, yes, yes, and no."

"Cool," His eyes sparkled with curiosity. "So can you teach me some cool magic powers now?"

I chuckled. Jeremy was thirsty for knowledge and to learn. He'd make for a good apprentice one day. "Sorry kiddo, I'm not much of a teacher. Plus my skillset wouldn't translate well. I'm a bit of a special case."

"Aww, but why?" Jeremy whined.

"Uh, it's a lot to explain," I said. "But don't worry, I have a friend not too far from here. I'll hit them up and see about getting you somewhere safe where you can learn more. But we should probably talk to your parents first."

Jeremy crossed his arms, scowling as he tried to look anywhere else but in front of him.

"What?" I asked.

"No parents, not unless you count Hank and Mallory," Jeremy grumbled.

Oh, that made some sense. "Foster parents?"

"Uh huh," Jeremy said. "They wouldn't even notice I was gone. They're too busy buying their drugs with the checks they get from the state."

I grimaced, that was unfortunate. But it wasn't the first time we'd come across neglectful foster parents who couldn't even be bothered to notice their foster child was no longer around. I filed that information away for later. I checked the time on my phone.

"It's getting late," I said. "Listen, go home tonight and I'll find you in a couple days once I've ironed out the details."

The sparkle returned to his eyes. "Really?"

"Really really," I nodded.

Chapter 2

I returned to the café the next day. I ordered my green tea, generously tipping the cashier, and took up my post where I had the day before. And the day before that, and the day before that as well. Sipping my tea, I unlocked my phone to go over the case files again. Twelve kids had seemingly vanished. I scrolled over their missing person profiles, hoping some earth-shattering detail would jump out at me.

They were all between the ages of twelve and sixteen and were misfits in one way or another. I noted instances of shoddy grades, trouble at home, and the occasional misdemeanor for good measure. And they'd all frequented the youth center. And that's why my ass was permanently imprinted on this chair.

Scanning through the files was starting to seriously depress me, so I swiped over to Reddit to see what nonsense people were spouting on there. It was a simple, sustainable routine that kept me occupied while I waited for something to happen.

Twenty minutes later, I unfortunately got my wish.

The boy from yesterday, Jeremy, was making his way up to the youth center when a man approached him. He wore an expensive, all-black suit and round-rimmed glasses with pitch black lenses. His dark hair and beard were neatly trimmed, but I couldn't make much else out from this distance. The man knelt down to speak at the boy's level. Words were exchanged and I wished super hearing was part of my skill set. Maybe I could ask someone at the Mystic Order to modify the enchantments woven into my clay body, throw in a few more useful skills for the covert parts of my job. Maybe something as cool as Matt Murdock's sonar vision. I noted that idea down for later. Jeremy seemed hesitant at first, but he gave the man a nod, and they started down the stairs.

God damn it, Jeremy.

I set my tea down and exited the café. An extreme case of déjà vu was hitting me right about now. Only this time, I wasn't confronting mortal bullies, but something presumably much more dangerous. They were headed in the direction of the alley and I feared that the man was about to kill the boy.

I hit the crosswalk button, keeping an eye on the duo the entire time. If there hadn't been so much traffic, I'd have said screw it and run across the street after them. But the last thing I needed was to get hit by an SUV before I got a chance to stop this guy. I was strong and durable, but a direct collision with a speeding car would take me out of the game as much as the next guy. Okay, maybe not as much, but it would still hurt and incapacitate me for at least an hour. That was time I simply didn't have.

The instant the light changed I was charging across the street for all I was worth. There was a lot of foot traffic and I struggled to keep Jeremy and the strange man in my line of sight. What I did know was they'd walked right past the alley. Where were they going?

"'Scuse me!" I shouted as I shoved past the meandering public. I was less than 100 feet away from Jeremy and the predator who'd lured him away.

I was closing in on them. Less than 50 feet now.

25 feet.

10 feet.

"Stop!" I yelled, loud enough so they could hear me.

Jeremy turned first, no doubt recognizing my voice. "Mr. Jacob?"

The man turned, smirking at me with a knowing look as he tipped his glasses down. The brown iris of his eyes suddenly disappeared and he extended his arm toward me faster than I could react. I skidded to a stop, hoping to confront him in a normal fashion. Supernatural types were rarely willing to expose their true natures out in the open.

This man was not one of those types.

His outstretched arm writhed and changed shape, forming into a fleshy tentacle with four rows of spiked barbs running down its length. The tentacle surged toward me and batted me away with surprising strength. I flew through the air, knocking over several innocent bystanders and falling hard on my back.

"Mr. Jacob!" Jeremy shouted in alarm.

I rose on my elbows just in time to see the man snatch the boy and haul him into an unmarked black car only ten feet behind him. Jeremy let out a panicked scream as the man shoved him into the backseat and then hopped into the passenger seat. The car's tires screeched and a moment later, the car had disappeared into the bustling traffic.

"Son of a bitch." I muttered.

I'd found my kidnapper, but I'd been foolish in my approach. Now he'd made off with Jeremy, and it'd be that much more challenging to find him. I rose to my feet, staring uselessly toward where I'd seen the car make its getaway.

I walked forward a few steps when something on the sidewalk caught my attention. It was a black sneaker. A boy's black sneaker. It had to be Jeremy's. He must've lost it when the man had grabbed him and shoved him into the car. I grinned. There was a chance I could still save Jeremy.

The tracking spell I used led me 15 miles out of town to Golden Gate Canyon State Park. The compass I was using as a conduit for the tracking spell eventually led me to a rather isolated area on one of the few roads that went through the park. I pulled my rental car off to the side of the road and got out.

I walked back and forth a few times just to confirm I'd followed the compass's directions correctly. I was certain that Jeremy and his kidnapper were somewhere nearby. Now there was just the mountainous task of finding them in this forest. I wasn't exactly sure what his kidnapper was, which made it harder to come up with a game plan. I locked the rental and began my trek into the forest. It was just past 5 o'clock, which meant I only had a few hours before darkness fell. Once the sun went down, I'd have little hope of finding Jeremy or the Agent Smith wannabe who had taken him. I had to find them quickly if I wanted to bring Jeremy back alive.

I stomped through the woods in the crisp, Colorado air. My golem physiology gave me near immunity to cold temperatures, but I couldn't help but think about how cold and scared Jeremy must be right now. The kid had seemed nice enough and clearly had a strong talent for magic, even if he didn't quite understand it just yet.

Beating myself up over the kid's plight wouldn't help me however. I considered possible strategies for dealing with his abductor. I could try my quicksand spell, but given that he could shapeshift, I had no doubt he could slip out of that particular bind. I had limited shapeshifting abilities of my own though. I could fashion my body into various melee weapons. And there weren't many problems that a giant stone club or axe couldn't solve. And there was plenty of natural earth that I could use to my advantage as well.

I looked down at the compass again, just to confirm I was still going in the right direction. I frowned at the cheap compass and sighed. The arrow was moving all over the place. Drat, something was interfering with the tracking spell. I tried to rack my brain for any information I could that tied all the factors together.

Jeremy and his magic, his shapeshifting kidnapper, the tracking spell's interference, and the forest itself. No matter how hard I thought about it, there was only one conclusion that added up. The only thing that tied those things together. Our kidnapper was a fae. Fae had a nasty habit of abducting kids. Whether it was to eat them or force them to live their lives out as changeling slaves. And if the kid had a magical talent? That was a welcome bonus. I hadn't brought any anti-fae equipment with me, which meant it was going to be a battle of brawn and wits. That is if I could find them.

I pocketed the useless compass and pondered my next move. The fae must've taken Jeremy back to its lair. Faeries, more often than not, lived in faerie mounds. They were portals to the faerie homeland. It went by many names, Fairyland, Otherworld, and Annwn, but the fae knew it as Tír na nÓg. If the kidnapper had already crossed over with Jeremy, that meant I'd most likely have to fight the fae on its home turf. And that would not be pleasant. Not at all.

Without a heavy dose of iron, my tracking spell would have no chance of tracking down Jeremy through the fairy mound's portal. I needed to devise a new strategy.

I was just about to pick a direction and start hiking again when I felt a surge of power rush through the air around me. I had only a second to react. I dove forward in an attempt to dodge the incoming attack. There was a detonation of energy somewhere behind me, the explosion flinging me farther than I'd intended. Unfortunately, the direction I'd chosen was right over the edge of a small cliff. I tumbled through the air, flipping head over heels, and landed hard. The wind was blown out of me right as the small of my back connected with a fallen log.

I let out a pained grunt but managed to roll with the blow, ending up on my hands and knees. I rose shakily to my feet, dusting off the dirt and debris that clung to me. I looked up the cliff and my eyes widened as my attacker came into view. They were a few inches shorter than me, but that was the only discernible detail I could make out. They were wearing a black cloak with silver stripes down the arms, torso, and hood. Despite the daylight still going strong, their face was cloaked entirely in shadow.

I narrowed my eyes, gathering up a smidgen of power as I planned to counterattack. I was pretty sure this wasn't the same person who'd kidnapped Jeremy, but maybe it was one of his allies. If that was the case, I was in trouble. The power they'd thrown around would've put some serious hurt on me if I hadn't sensed it in time.

I prepared for the worst as the cloaked figure raised one hand into the air and began to gather power.

Black Cloak flung another blast of emerald energy at me, but I was ready this time. I raised my arm and as I did, a half-dome of magically enhanced clay expanded from my forearm. The energy blast pushed me half a foot back but otherwise bounced harmlessly off my shield. I reached forward with my other hand, golden green energy coating my arm up to my elbow.

"Terrae Motus!" I shouted.

The cliff under Black Cloak's feet shook violently and the loose earth gave way. Black Cloak let out a startled breath as the ground shifted and slid out from under them. They struggled to keep their balance as they slid down to my level. I didn't give them the chance to recover. I charged forward, my forearm and fist expanding to nearly three times its size, taking on an earthen texture. I closed the distance in less than a second and swung as hard as I could with my giant stone fist.

Unfortunately, Black Cloak recovered faster than I'd expected. They saw my swing coming and, with both hands, formed a nebulous cloud of emerald energy. It was too late to pull my strike so I committed to it, hoping the kinetic energy and my strength would be enough to power through. Oh how wrong I was. When my fist made contact with the green cloud of energy, it suddenly slowed to a snail's pace.

My eyebrows shot up in surprise. I took a step forward to keep my balance and tried to pull my fist free, but it only slowed further. Whoever Black Cloak was, they were strong. They'd created a cloud of slowed-down time. That was heavyweight magic and if I'd known they were capable of this, I would have thought twice about fighting back instead of just running away.

Black Cloak cocked their head, extended their hand out until they were nearly touching my chest, and hissed out an incantation. Their signature emerald energy exploded forth and struck me in the chest, sending me tumbling away.

I hit the ground rolling, but I managed to use that momentum to my advantage. I got my feet under me and skidded to a halt twenty feet away. I gritted my teeth as I stood. I retracted my shield in favor of a second oversized fist.

"I don't have time for this!" I growled. "I've got a kid to save!"

Black Cloak, who'd been preparing another magical strike, suddenly stopped. They lowered their guard slightly but kept the emerald energy at the ready. I narrowed my eyes in response.

"You're looking for a lost child?" Black Cloak asked, their voice was distorted slightly. It made it hard to tell if they were man, woman, or somewhere in between.

"Yeah, what about it?" I snapped.

Black Cloak dispersed the gathered energy, holding their hands up placatingly. I didn't return the gesture, holding my giant fists at the ready in case I needed to bash their head in. Nothing beats the giant fist. Okay, maybe clouds of chronomancy beat giant fists, but that was besides the point.

"We have a common enemy then." Black Cloak said. "I'm hunting the thing that's abducting the children."

I cocked an eyebrow at that. "Is that right? Then why did you attack me?"

"From a distance, I couldn't tell what exactly you were. Only that you had a magical aura," Black Cloak explained. "It wasn't until you started using golem magic that I realized you were not my target."

"Yeah, far from it," I said. "The kidnapper is some kind of shapeshifter. Looked human up until his arm morphed into a spiky tentacle and smacked me across the concrete."

"It's a doppelgänger, just about the most notorious kind of fae shapeshifter you can find," Black Cloak explained. "But it's not the one responsible; it acts only as an agent for the real culprit."

Great, so I had more than one bad guy to worry about. Doppelgängers were nasty pieces of work and extremely rare. They could shapeshift into perfect copies of just about anything so long as they had enough time to get a good handle on the details. But there were no records of what a doppelgänger looked like in its true form. They were hard to find and even harder to study.

I considered my options for a moment. If Black Cloak was right about the doppelgänger serving a master, then I was outnumbered. I eyed the mysterious stranger.

"We seem to have a common enemy," I began. "We owe it to those kids to work together. What do you think?"

Black Cloak stood still, saying nothing. With that hood up, it was hard to tell what they were thinking. But after a moment, their hood twitched forward in a nod.

"Very well, your assistance could prove useful." Black Cloak said.

"Forever the sidekick", a bitter, darker corner of my psyche muttered. But I shooed the thought away. What mattered was saving Jeremy and stopping the doppelgänger and its master from taking any more kids.

"Alright then, let's get moving," I said. "What should I call you, by the way? 'Black Cloak' just doesn't have much of a ring to it."

Black Cloak seemed to consider the question for a moment. "You may call me Wraith."

Then they reached up and lowered their hood, revealing the face of a beautiful woman. She was a stunning sight and couldn't have been older than twenty-five. She had piercing hazel eyes that seemed to shift between gray, blue, and green as the light danced between the treetops. She had a soft, round face that would have detracted from their lethality if I hadn't already seen her in action. Her most startling feature was her snow-white hair, which she kept tied back in a long ponytail that had miraculously stayed hidden until now. For reasons I couldn't quite place, there was something familiar about her.

Chapter 3

Wraith seemed very accustomed to tracking down the fae. She'd gathered some random debris from the forest floor, including an old stick, a dandelion, and an acorn. In addition to Jeremy's shoe, Wraith whipped up a tracking spell that seemed to lock on perfectly. The odd assortment of the forest's children combined with the young boy's shoe glowed with emerald light. Bands of energy flowed above the spell and coalesced into the shape of a glowing hummingbird. The bird construct fluttered furiously, darting around in the air.

"Huh, never seen a tracking spell work quite like that." I said.

"Magic works in many ways," Wraith said.

On cue, the hummingbird seemed to lock in on its target and darted into the forest. Wraith moved soundlessly to follow it. I grabbed Jeremy's shoe and did the same.

I was still wary of Wraith. She showed up out of nowhere and happened to be on the trail of the same fae as I was. I couldn't quite place it, but their magic was somehow different from a normal wizard's. And this whole time, Wraith had yet to take off their hood, opting to keep their face hidden in shadow. Normal people didn't go around shrouded in shadow and hunting fae. Just what was this Wraith character hiding?

Wraith seemed to move effortlessly through the uneven terrain, a trait she could only have acquired by growing up in a forest like this. I mean, I supposed she could've been one flavor of vampire or another, but I had never heard of a vampire who'd be invested in saving children instead of eating them. They were a wizard, but I highly doubted she was associated with the Mystic Order. Otherwise, I should've known she was coming and there'd be no need to hide their identity.

After another twenty minutes or so of walking, I was starting to grow impatient.

"Any idea where your little birdie is taking us?" I asked.

"To the faerie's lair, of course," Wraith replied matter of factly.

I sighed. "I know that. I was looking for something a little more specific."

Wraith looked over their shoulder for a moment. Then turned back around and kept heading in the direction that the hummingbird was leading us. Annoyance bubbled up inside of me. I jogged to catch up to Wraith, my movements fueled by the growing impatience, annoyance, and anger that had been building since Jeremy was kidnapped.

"Hey!" I snapped, grabbing Wraith by the shoulder. I spun them around to face me, staring hard into the void of their hood. "Would it kill you to give me a little more information? Are we close? What should I be looking out for? What's your deal with the fae? Anything would suffice at this rate! And another thi—!"

Wraith thrust their hand over my mouth, shutting me up. With her free hand, she motioned for me to be quiet. I frowned. Wraith turned and pointed to the hummingbird, who'd stopped advancing into the forest. Instead, the glowing green avian was circling over a small hole in the side of a pile of forest debris. It was made of sticks, stones, leaves, and other materials you'd expect to find in a heavily wooded area.

"We're here," Wraith whispered. "If I remove my hand, can I trust you to keep quiet long enough for us to sneak through the faerie's defenses?"

I nodded and Wraith removed her hand. I eyed the pile of debris with a skeptical look. "That's the faerie mound? It's freaking tiny."

"Looks can be deceiving," Wraith said. "Faerie mounds are merely gateways to Tír na nÓg. In this instance, I suspect they lead to my target's personal demesne."

"So we're gonna bust into this guy's house and punch him in the nose?" I asked, trying to confirm the game plan.

"You are not one for the subtle approach, are you?" Wraith said, a hint of skepticism in their voice.

"You should see my best friend," I chuckled.

"I have no idea what kind of defenses or opposition we can expect once we're through the portal." Wraith explained. "It's possible that the target could have allies waiting on the other side, just waiting for us to come through so they can get the jump on us."

"Seems kinda direct for a guy operating through a doppelgänger proxy." I countered.

Wraith cocked their head. "Fair point."

"But you do have a point." I said. "Best to go in slow and cautious."

"I'm glad I could persuade you."

"And once we've dealt with the advance guard, we go hog wild on the rest." I grinned broadly.

"I'd hate to meet your friend." Wraith said flatly.

The entrance to the faerie mound was small, barely two feet in diameter. I'm not Hulk-sized or anything like that, but I'm a pretty big guy. I wouldn't be much of a golem if I didn't have some mass to throw around. This was one of the few times where it proved to be a disadvantage. I grunted as I shimmied one shoulder through at a time. In the process, I'd inadvertently pinned my arms to my side. I let out a heavy sigh.

"A little help?" I grunted.

Wraith had already crossed through. Their arms crossed as she looked down at me. I wasn't sure if that shadowed hood was hiding amusement or impatience. I didn't really care, I just wanted to get out of the stupid hole.

Wraith waved a cloaked hand in my general direction. The earth shifted slightly just before several tendril-like roots emerged. They wrapped around my shoulders and under my armpits. With a couple of hard tugs, I was through the hole in one piece. I couldn't say the same for my dignity, but that was besides the point.

I cleared my throat once before saying, "Thanks."

"Forget it," Wraith said dismissively and began to take a look at our surroundings.

I did as well, taking notice of where we'd ended up for the first time. Wraith had been right. We weren't in Kansas anymore. Or anywhere on Earth for that matter. Tír na nÓg, the land of the faeries, was a domain that made up a sizable chunk of The World Yonder. After all, the fae were the largest, the most widespread and the most diverse faction in the supernatural world.

Tír na nÓg was beautiful and extremely varied in its environments. But from what I could tell, we hadn't arrived in Fairyland proper. We were in a dank cave, the walls made up of packed dirt. Patches of glowing moss decorated the earthen walls, providing soft light to see by. Tree roots snaked through the ground, the walls, and the ceiling, but there wasn't much else in terms of scenery. I looked passed Wraith, and noted the cave seemed to go deeper than my eyes could see.

"Kind of a drab living situation, I must say," I said, still looking around.

"The kidnapper is a slippery weasel of a creature. A dark, dank place like this suits them well. No doubt protected by hundreds of individual wards and spells to keep intruders away, except for this entrance. The doppelgänger wouldn't be able to get through otherwise." Wraith said.

That made enough sense. The faerie mound didn't even have any sort of glamour or "look away" spells protecting it. I was curious how many people had disappeared down this particular rabbit hole over the years. I'd have to make sure we sealed off this faerie mound after we'd handled business.

Wraith glided deeper into the tunnel. I followed after them, careful not to get tripped up over the exposed roots and small boulders. While the tunnel was dark and secluded, it was still pretty cool to visit a place of such vibrant magic. I could feel it as a tangible substance in the air, the ambient magic of Tír na nÓg brushing against my own. It felt familiar somehow, but I couldn't quite place it.

We walked for a bit longer, though I wasn't quite sure how long. Time worked differently in Tír na nÓg and The World Yonder as a whole. Five minutes here could be twenty seconds or three days back home. No one had nailed down a way to keep track of the constantly changing time differential.

I nearly bowled over Wraith before I'd realized she'd stopped moving. She held out her arm to the side, blocking me from progressing. I gave Wraith a sideways glance.

"What's wrong? Why'd we stop?" I said after a moment of silence.

"There's something in the tunnel." Wraith whispered.

I swung my head around, trying to nail down what she could have been talking about. "I don't see anyth—"

The tunnel shook.

Dirt fell from the ceiling. Wraith and I went absolutely still. A tremor shook the tunnel again and more dirt and dust fell.

"What the hell is that?" I asked.

Wraith's body tensed. "I just realized what kind of tunnel this is."

The ground erupted in front of us. I grabbed Wraith around the waist and leaped backwards as something emerged from the tunnel floor. I managed to land on my feet, skidding across the dirt floor. Wraith freed themselves roughly from my grip and I could feel their glare from underneath the hood.

"What, did you wanna get eaten by whatever that thing is?" I growled, annoyed with their hostility.

Wraith ignored me, though. Her attention was on the creature emerging from the ground. Once I got a good look at it, I realized exactly what it was. It was a Wyrm, a type of dragon with no legs or wings to speak of. Its white scales and piercing green eyes added to its intimidating appearance. Its head and neck stuck out of the ground and nearly brushed the ceiling. Judging from that, it was probably somewhere near eighty feet long.

Wraith extended herm arm towards the angry wyrm, glowing emerald magic gathering around her hand. She shouted a word and six giant tree roots burst out of the ground, surging towards the wyrm. Two of the roots wrapped around the creature's snout but were quickly dispatched by its raw strength. The wyrm hissed and roared as it emerged further from the ground. The four remaining roots whipped and snapped towards the wyrm, attempting to keep it at bay. But it was a losing battle. The wyrm snapped its jaws around one of the roots, tearing it in half and tossing it away. It'd only be a matter of time before the wyrm broke through our defenses.

"It's going to get through!" I shouted.

"Got any better ideas?" Wraith shot back.

I grunted. Truthfully, I didn't. But we'd have to do something if we didn't want to become wyrm food. I concentrated, golden green light forming around my fist. In a flash, my hand shifted into a stone mace.

"Keep it distracted!" I yelled.

I charged forward while the wyrm was still engaged with the remaining roots. The wyrm screeched in rage but didn't seem to notice me as I flanked it. The thing was huge and normally I'd think twice before charging straight at such a behemoth. But there were kids in danger, and no overgrown rat snake was going to stand in my way.

I shouted a battle cry as I leaped towards the wyrm, my mace arm at the ready. I swung as hard as I could, striking the wyrm across the face for all I was worth. The beast let out a startled cry as it crashed into the cavern wall. I landed on its neck and drove my mace hand directly into its exposed eye. Lime green fluid exploded out from its destroyed eye and it let out a pained cry. Before I could celebrate, the wyrm spasmed in pain and rage, sending me tumbling into the opposite wall.

The wyrm swiveled its head until its remaining eye locked onto me. Pure rage filled its lopsided gaze and its charged straight for me, giant maw wide open and ready to consume its prey. Moments before I became wyrm chow, a bolt of green energy struck the creature's head, causing it to recoil away.

Wraith flung another bolt of power at the wyrm, and then another. Each attack striking the wyrm and driving it further back. The wyrm let out a final screech of defiance, but it was on the retreat. It began to slither towards the hole from which it emerged.

"Don't let it get away!" Wraith growled.

I nodded, rushing towards the creature. I grabbed the end of its tail, holding on for all I was worth. I felt magic running through me as I exerted the entirety of my golem strength. But I was no match for this thing's raw strength. My sneakers kicked up dirt as I slid across the ground, while the wyrm desperately tried to get away.

"Just hold it for a second longer!" Wraith shouted.

I couldn't see what they were up to, but they'd better be quick about it. I could feel the wyrm slipping free. If I lost it now, the creature would escape and be free to cause us problems later on.

A flash of movement startled me and made me nearly lose my grip. Two dark shapes crossed over the wyrm through the air, landing near the creature's head on opposite sides. They lunged at the wyrm's neck. I saw a flash of tooth and claw, and a second later, green blood erupted like a geyser from the wyrm's neck. The wyrm let out a final, pained cry before crashing to the ground, less than ten feet away from its escape route.

I wiped away some of the green eye fluid that had exploded onto me as I went to investigate just what had taken the wyrm down. Wraith strolled alongside me as two very large wolves with black fur went to greet my mysterious companion. No, not wolves. They were vargrs, giant faerie wolves. They primarily thrived in the dark forests of the Unseelie courts, but I'd heard of them being found in the Seelie forests as well.

The wolves greeted Wraith like a dog would its master, pushing her hands on top of their heads. Wraith scratched their necks affectionately and looked towards me.

I eyed Wraith and their lupine companions with skepticism. I'd never heard of vargrs, or any fae creature for that matter, serving under a wizard master. Wraith was just full of surprises.

"Quite the trick," I said, not bothering to hide the wariness in my voice.

"I didn't dare risk calling them out sooner. They wouldn't have fared well in a fair fight against the wyrm. But once we had it on the run, it was the perfect opening for them to go for the kill." Wraith explained.

That didn't tell me much about how she'd bound the vargrs to her will, but I didn't have time to ask questions. Just then, I heard a panicked boy's cry from somewhere deeper in the tunnel.

"Jeremy!" I shouted. I ran past the wyrm corpse, delving deeper into the tunnel.

Chapter 4

Wraith wasn't far behind me, an impressive feat considering how fast I could move when I leaned into my golem strength. I could hear the grunts and growls of Wraith's vargrs as they followed close behind. Eventually, a stone altar came into view. I skidded to a stop as I took in the scene. The altar was on a raised platform, with half a dozen steps leading up to a stone table. Jeremy had been beaten and bound in rope. One of his eyes was blackened and swollen shut and he had a nasty cut on his lip that oozed blood. Upon seeing me, Jeremy's uninjured eye glittered with hope.

"Mister Jacob, you came to rescue me!" Jeremy said. I had to hand it to him. Despite his situation, the kid sounded cheerful and optimistic.

"Don't worry Jeremy, I'm gonna get you out of here!" I shouted back. I turned to Wraith. "Watch my back, I'm gonna get the kid out of there."

Wraith tilted her head forward in acknowledgement.

Before I could even get close to the kid though, a figure emerged from behind one of the stone pillars. It was the handsome gentleman who'd kidnapped Jeremy in the first place. In reality, I knew he wasn't a handsome gentleman, but a doppelgänger in disguise.

"Disappointing," The doppelgänger said. "I'd expected you to arrive much earlier. I suppose it all worked out though. The ritual is nearly ready."

Emerald power erupted from under Wraith's sleeves as they took a battle-ready stance. "Where is your master?"

"Ah, my master was expecting you as well." The doppelgänger said. "This presents a rare opportunity. It isn't every day that my master will be able to eliminate a pawn of both the Mystic Order and the Seelie courts."

I gave Wraith a sideways glance. I assumed that I was the Mystic Order agent in this case, which meant that Wraith had some connection to the Seelie courts. The pieces of the puzzle were starting to click into place. But I had to stay focused. Jeremy was still in very real danger. I'd have time to question her once the boy was safe and sound.

"Hand over the boy, doppelgänger, and you and your master can go free!" I growled. Golden green energies gathered around my fists. "Resist, and I'll destroy you both myself."

"I'd like to see you try," a new voice said.

A figure shimmered into existence, standing over Jeremy's bound form. He was gorgeous—even I could admit that. He was tall, around 6'5", and had long, blonde hair. He wore a tailored forest green three-piece suit. His green eyes glimmered despite the faint lighting of the cave.

"Cathal," Wraith hissed.

"Ah, if it isn't the Eclipse Druid," Cathal said, a tone of disdain and superiority coating his voice. "A pleasure to finally meet you."

"Save me the pleasantries, Cathal," Wraith growled. "You've gotten sloppy. King Oberon has become all too privy to your unauthorized abductions. I'm to bring him your head."

Wait a freaking moment. What had Cathal called her? The Eclipse Druid? That answered several of my questions regarding my enigmatic companion. How she'd been able to track Jeremy through the fae's defenses, the strange magic they used, and the vargrs under their command. Wraith was a druid, a mortal practitioner who specialized in the manipulation of fae magic. Not only that, but she seemed to be loyal to the Seelie courts, considering the mention of King Oberon. Oberon was a major figure among the Seelie courts, he was the ruling monarch of the Spring Court and the husband of Queen Titania. If Wraith truly was a servant of the faerie king, that meant that she was a heavy hitter for sure. And I'd found myself in the middle of inter-fae conflict.

"Oberon is a fool who is too lenient with the cattle. Once my plan is complete and I've fed on enough mortal wizards, my power will rival his! And I'll take the throne of the Spring Court for myself!" Cathal said triumphantly.

Judging by his unreal beauty and arrogance, I assumed that Cathal was one of the sídhe, a nobleman among the fae. His supernatural good looks would be rivaled only by his proficiency in magic. That meant he was way out of my league. But Wraith had probably been prepared to handle him.

"Can you take him?" I whispered.

"Take care of the doppelgänger. Cathal is mine." Wraith said, ignoring my question.

And that's when all hell broke loose.

Wraith unleashed a bolt of emerald energy at Cathal. The sídhe drew a silver rapier and flicked it through the air at the emerald blast. The blast split in half, sailing harmlessly past the sídhe. Wraith hissed and charged toward Cathal.

That left me to deal with the doppelgänger, who wasted no time in closing the distance between us. His arms blurred and changed into twin tendrils with serrated teeth-like spines. He slashed at me with the tentacles, but I danced just out of his reach. My arms glowed with golden green energy as they took on a clay-like texture and expanded into giant fists. Dodging another swipe of his spined tentacles, I rushed forward and slugged the doppelgänger across the jaw. He flashed a maniacal grin and spit out a tooth. Before I realized what was happening, the doppelgänger had wrapped one of his tentacles around me and flung me into the cavern wall.

I grunted from the impact and slumped to the ground in a daze.

"Surrender now, and I'll make your death quick," the doppelgänger taunted.

"Where'd you hear that one? Game of Thrones?" I growled in response. I shouted a word of power and struck the ground in front of me.

Several sharp rocks erupted from underneath the doppelgänger. But the peon was faster than I expected. He balanced the tip of his toe on the tallest rock spike as it erupted from the ground and used the momentum to leap away to a safe distance.

I took a moment to see how Wraith was handling her opponent. Wraith and her vargrs worked like a true wolf pack, cornering their prey. One of the vargrs would lash out with its fangs, forcing Cathal to dance out of the way. But that left him open for a follow-up attack from the other vargr and Wraith. The remaining vargr rushed past Cathal, lashing out with its claws. I saw perfectly red blood fly through the air as the vargr's strike landed true. Wraith followed up with a swift strike from a silver chain that she'd produced from somewhere underneath her cloak. The silver struck Cathal across the face and left scalding burn marks across his perfect complexion.

In a rage, Cathal yelled out in a language I didn't recognize. A gout of flame flew from his sword and struck Wraith square in the chest. Wraith tumbled down the stairs of the altar, landing in a heap at the bottom of the steps. Wraith didn't let the fire spell keep her down for long though. She leapt back into action, swinging her chain in a mesmerizing pattern as she prepared a counterattack.

I'd been so distracted with Wraith's fight that I'd completely forgotten about the doppelgänger. I cursed at myself, because as I turned my attention back to it, I realized I was in trouble. The doppelgänger's form had just finished shifting. Before where a handsome man had been, now stood a nearly eight-foot tall minotaur.

"Now that's just unfair," I sighed.

In his new form, the doppelgänger let out a bovine roar of challenge. His hooved feet stamped the ground once and then he charged straight for me. Screw it, it was time to see just how strong I really was. I let out a battle cry as I charged to meet the oncoming minotaur. I set my shoulder into a football player's tackle, bracing for impact as we closed the distance between each other. I kept my center of gravity low and hoped for the best.

Luckily for my shoulder, my plan paid off. I struck low, right in the doppel-taur's groin. As we collided, I heaved for all I was worth and sent the beast flying overhead as I rushed by. I skidded to a stop in a three-point stance, pivoting to watch the doppel-taur crash to the ground.

I had the doppelgänger on the ropes, now I just had to finish it. My hand morphed into a mace as I ran towards the fallen doppelgänger. Once I was through with this thing, I could assist Wraith in her fight against Cathal. I leaped into the air, raising my mace hand above my head as I prepared to bring it down on the doppelgänger's head.

But the doppel-taur wasn't as stunned as I'd initially thought. He swung his big, meaty paw at me and slammed me into the ground with all of his strength. I grunted as the impact blew the wind out of me. Having to worry about breathing when I was supposed to be a supernatural sentinel seemed like a scam, but I tried not to focus on that train of thought. I wheezed as I desperately tried to get my wits about me and air into my lungs.

The doppel-taur sauntered over to me, brimming with confidence as he came to stand over me. "Gotta say you're tough, little golem." He said in a deep, baritone voice. "But you should never have come here." With that, the doppel-taur raised one of his hooves over my head, preparing to crush me with all of his weight.

I acted without thinking, punching towards the doppel-taur as I wheezed out a spell. "*Gladius!*"

A spike of rock and earth burst out from the ground beside my head and struck through the doppel-taur's face. Pale blood exploded out of his head and rained down on me. The doppelgänger's body went limp as it began to revert to its true form. In its true form, the doppelgänger was a pale, skinny humanoid. I estimated it was about four feet tall, but otherwise had no defining features. I couldn't quite make out its face, since I'd impaled it with a giant rock. What I was sure of was that the thing was most certainly dead.

"One down," I rasped. "One to go."

Wraith let out a pained cry. My gaze darted over to her. She'd fallen to the ground and Cathal was engaged in battle with her vargrs. To call it a battle was being generous to the vargrs. He'd picked up one of the vargrs by the scruff and was swinging it like a club at its twin. The remaining vargr danced out of the way of Cathal's swings and responded with a lunge, its fangs gleaming in the low light. Cathal had been expecting the attack and quickly redirected his swing so that the two vargrs collided in midair. He let go at the end of his swing and sent both vargrs flying through the air. They landed in a pained heap at my feet as I stood up.

I knelt to check on the vargrs. They were alive, but I could feel some ribs out of place in one and the other's left foreleg was bent at an odd angle. The vargrs wouldn't be doing any fighting anytime soon. I decided there was nothing I could do for them at the moment and that my efforts were best spent helping Wraith. I hopped up the stairs two at a time as I rushed to help the druid take down the rogue sídhe.

Wraith spun like a breakdancer, the chain whipping out dangerously. It slashed Cathal across his shins. The sídhe cried out in pain as he toppled over. Wraith rose to her feet, holding the chain taut. Green druid magic began to flow along the chain's length as Wraith stood over Cathal.

"I would have let you come quietly, Cathal," Wraith said. Then she smiled. "But I'm glad you decided to fight back. It's not often I get to have any fun."

I gave Wraith another odd look. There was a hint of murderous glee in her voice that I didn't care much for. She was enjoying this. I turned back to Cathal. "You give up, glitter pants?"

Cathal let out a bitter chuckle. "Oh far from it."

The sídhe blurred into motion. I only had a second to react. I raised my arm just in time to deflect a slash from his rapier. If I'd been human, the sídhe blade would have cut my arm clean off. Thank you, golem durability. Cathal spun and slashed at Wraith, but she caught the blade in her chain and jerked it out of his hands. Cathal cursed in an unknown tongue and spun. Before he'd completed the spin, he'd vanished.

Wraith and I went back-to-back, trying to look everywhere at once. I saw a flash of silver rush past me and then a burst of kinetic energy sent me tumbling sideways down the steps. Cathal appeared a moment later, half a dozen steps behind Wraith, his rapier in hand. He rushed at her back but Wraith was quick on her feet, she turned to meet the sídhe and held out her chain defensively. The silver rapier clanged against the chain. But before Wraith could tangle it up again with her chain, Cathal pulled it away.

Wraith let go of one end of the chain as it surged with emerald power and swung it overhead at Cathal. He deflected it and lunged. I saw a flash of scarlet as he slashed through Wraith's cloak and into her shoulder. She let out a pained grunt but extended her good arm and shouted a word. A bolt of green energy exploded and sent Cathal skidding back across the stone.

Cathal hissed out a word and slashed his rapier through the air. A blade of fire flew towards Wraith, but she called up an emerald cloud. As the fire made contact, it immediately slowed to a snail's pace. Cathal seemed surprised by this. While Wraith had called up the cloud of slowed time to defend herself, I realized it was also a distraction. Two vargrs blurred into view and slashed their teeth across the back of Cathal's legs.

I turned to where I'd left the two vargrs from before. Sure enough, they were still there. Which meant that Wraith had a whole pack of them under her command. The two vargrs worked in tandem to keep Cathal off balance, but it was a losing battle. The sídhe was fast and smart.

Cathal let out a bellow of rage as he swiped his blade. I heard a pained yowl from one of the vargrs as Cathal separated one of its legs at the elbow. Wraith swung her chain and I saw electricity crackle down its length. She flung it towards Cathal while he was distracted. It wrapped around him in a flash, and electricity surged into the sídhe's body. He went rigid and dropped his blade. Cathal fell to his knees, still bound in the silver chain.

Wraith began to reel the chain in, dragging Cathal's limp form towards her as he moaned and groaned. I eyed her warily as I approached. The vargr that had kept all its limbs followed Cathal's limp form closely, offering warning growls and flashes of its deadly fangs.

With the chain wrapped around one hand, Wraith went and picked up Cathal's rapier. "Huh, a fine weapon. I'll take it off your hands, Cathal. Seeing how you'll no longer need it."

Wraith tucked the rapier somewhere in her cloak and returned her attention to the bound sídhe. "King Oberon will be happy to see you returned."

"No..." Cathal croaked weakly. "You can't bring me back there."

I had a moment of clarity, remembering that Jeremy still lay bound on the stone table. Putting the situation between the druid and Cathal at the back of my mind, I hurried over to Jeremy.

With one hard tug, I ripped apart the ropes that had bound him and helped the kid sit up. "You okay, kid?"

Jeremy seemed a bit out of it, but he gave me his best smile. "Yes sir, Mister Jacob. That was awesome! How'd you do all that stuff with your arms and the rocks and stuff?"

I smiled. "Don't worry, kid, given some time, you may be able to pull off some pretty neat tricks of your own."

Chapter 5

We emerged from the faerie mound. It was a little awkward to get Cathal through since he'd been wrapped up in the silver chain, but we all managed. Night had fallen during our field trip to fairyland. It'd be annoying as hell to find our way back with only the moon to light our way. Jeremy was better off than he looked. If we'd taken a little longer, Cathal would have killed him and taken the kid's raw magical talent for himself. I wondered if it was possible if he'd be able to gather enough power to rival a fae lord like Oberon. Good thing we wouldn't have to worry about that.

I turned to Wraith. "Thank you for your help."

"Think nothing of it. I didn't do it for you or the kid, only in service of King Oberon." Wraith said flatly.

I raised an eyebrow. "Uh huh, right." I nodded my head towards Cathal. "So what happens to him?"

"That is up to my king." Wraith said.

I had an idea what was in store for Cathal. Faeries could hold a grudge, nevermind a fae lord such as Oberon. I pitied Cathal, but only a little. After all, he'd killed all those kids. A whole lot of good it did him, though; Wraith had taken care of him pretty easily. He must've been low on the totem pole from the start.

That's when my phone rang. I frowned, wondering who'd be calling me at this time of night. I held up one finger, signaling Wraith to wait a moment and pulled out my phone.

Displayed on the screen was the name of my best friend, Tobias Leight. I frowned, wondering why he'd be calling at this time of night. Then I slid my finger across the screen and held the phone up to my ear. "Uh, hello."

"Jacob, it's Tobias. Oh crap, sorry! Did I wake you?" Tobias said, his voice a little rough.

I yawned. "No, sorry. Just been a little busy and wore myself out."

"Sorry, it's been a long couple of days and my head's a bit scrambled," Tobias said sheepishly. "I forgot to check the time before calling."

I yawned again, not realizing how tired I really was. "Really, it's no big deal. What's up?"

Tobias began ranting like a madman. He caught me up on a brewing gang war between Seattle's vampire factions. In his flurry of words, I caught details of a biblical artifact and his uncle, Bishop, having been captured during the conflict.

Finally he said, "And now, here we are."

I rubbed the back of my head and puffed out a breath. "Vampires, man. I leave for two months and you find a way to get this deep into trouble."

It figured my best friend would find a way to get mixed up with those blood suckers. Not to mention the emotion or soul suckers.

"Yeah, which is why I could use you back here." Tobias said. I could detect the desperation in his voice. He was scared and not sure what to do next. Whatever exactly was going on back home, it definitely had rattled him.

"While I appreciate your confidence in me," I began. "Why don't you just ask the Mystic Order for help?"

"I plan to." Tobias clarified. "But I don't really know anyone from the Order that well. If I'm going into this, I want to make sure I have someone with my best interests at heart by my side."

"Just say you don't trust the Order." I said with a grin.

"I'm not saying I trust them or don't, but I definitely trust you."

"Fair enough." I relented. "Okay, my work out here has pretty much reached its end, anyways. I just have to handle something before I go. I can be back in Seattle by the morning."

Tobias let out a sigh of relief. "Thanks. It means a lot. I'll see you in the morning."

"Get some rest." I told him before ending the call.

"Seems like you have more work to do." Wraith said, brushing a strand of her white hair out of her face.

"Uh huh, a golem's work never ends." I said. "Seriously, thanks again."

"Don't mention it." Wraith said. "If you'll excuse me, I have to take this trash back to the Spring Court, so he can face justice. Perhaps we'll meet again, under better circumstances."

Before I could say anything further, Wraith simply disappeared with her quarry. One moment, there they were. The next, they were gone. I turned to Jeremy, who seemed pretty chipper despite the ordeal he'd gone through.

"What happens to me now?" He asked.

I knelt down so that we were face to face. "I could take you back to the community center. But you have talent, kid, and someday you could be a real, honest to God, wizard."

Jeremy's eyes widened. "Really?"

I nodded. "Really. But I won't bore you with the details. I know someone in town who can help you."

With that said and done, we began our long hike back to my rental car. It took us a while, but eventually we made it back. I helped the kid into the car and began the drive back to Golden. I checked the time, it was a quarter to midnight. By the time we got back into town, it'd be nearly 12:30. Hopefully, the person I was taking Jeremy to see would be awake.

Jeremy fell asleep almost immediately. The kid had a rough day, so I couldn't blame him. I was pretty much taxed myself. Soon enough, we'd arrived at our destination. I left Jeremy to sleep in the car for a few minutes longer while I went up to the front door of the cozy little home.

I knocked on the door, hard enough to be heard without sounding too aggressive. After a couple of minutes and several knocks, I heard the door unlock and it swung open. Inside was a frail old woman, with dark wrinkled skin and an afro of curly gray hair.

"Hilda, it's good to see you," I said. "Sorry about the time."

Hilda gave me a warm smile as she finished tying her robe. "Not a problem dearie, the Order told me to expect you sometime soon."

"You sure you're up for fostering this kid?" I asked.

"Wouldn't be the first troublesome young wizard I took under my wing." Hilda beamed. She tilted her head to the car. "Is that him?"

I turned to look over my shoulder. Jeremy had gotten out of the car, a nervous look on his face. "Who's she?" He said.

I smiled broadly, showing my teeth. "This is Hilda, Jeremy. She's a hedge witch, and she's agreed to look after you while you learn more about what you can do."

Hilda held out a hand, her smile still on full display. "Your name's Jeremy, is it? I've been expecting you, dearie. Would you like to come inside? I have food and a warm bed waiting for you."

Jeremy's unswollen eye lit up at that. He ran over to Hilda and took her hand.

"You did good, Jacob," Hilda said. "I'll see to it that all the proper paperwork is in order for young Jeremy here."

"Thank you Hilda," I said.

"Would you like to stay the night? There's enough room and food for one more." She offered.

I held up a hand. "I wish I could, but I just got a call. I need to head back to Seattle. Sounds like trouble's a-brewin'." I explained.

Hilda smiled. "Very well, dearie,"

I turned to leave. Before I could take even one step away, a voice rang out.

"Mister Jacob, wait!"

I turned back just in time to see Jeremy leap towards me, wrapping his arms around my neck. "Thank you Mister Jacob! But will I ever see you again?"

I knelt so that he could stand. Truth was, I didn't have enough strength left in me to support him. "Maybe someday, kiddo. And what'd I tell you about calling me mister? It's just Jacob."

"Right, Jacob," Jeremy nodded. "Well I hope you get home safe. And I'll see you soon."

With that, Hilda took Jeremy's hand once more and led him inside. "Bye, dearie," She said.

I waved and smiled at the pair before she closed the door.

Right, with that settled, it was about time I got home. It seemed my best friend had stirred up some trouble back in the Rainy City, and he needed my help.

And there was no way I was going to leave him hanging.

Tobias Leight Saves Christmas

'Twas the night before Christmas, when all through the house

Not a creature was stirring, not even the dog, Scout.

When one young wizard, after a holiday bash

Awoke from his slumber, as he heard a crash.

This story takes place on Christmas Eve, the year after *Fang Wars*. If you haven't read *Fallen Son* or *Fang Wars*, I suggest you read those first and come back later.

Chapter 6

I shot up in bed as I heard the loud crash. I looked at the clock, two minutes to midnight. Just great. I was still completely exhausted from the Williams family Christmas party. The noise was probably nothing, right? Some guy drunk on eggnog hit a stop sign or something. That made sense. I considered waking my uncle to come investigate with me. But then I remembered that he and Scout were out of town on Order business, and wouldn't be back until the morning.

But something didn't seem quite right. It was like a tingle in the air. That tingle, I recognized it. There was magic at work. I grabbed my lone eskrima from the floor next to my bed, its twin having been destroyed the year before. Just what I needed. I tiptoed out of my room, trying to listen for further disturbance. I snuck down the stairs, our modest

Christmas tree shining with lights. The crystalline star that rested on top reflected the light into a brilliant display of color that bathed the living room. But my attention was on our front door. Someone was outside, that much I could tell. And even though I couldn't hear exactly what they were saying, I could recognize a disgruntled tirade from a mile away. My uncle was famous for those.

Someone was outside my door and pissed. I stood in front of my door, wearing only pajamas. I was dreading the incoming blast of winter air almost more than I was dreading the confrontation I was about to find myself in.

Gripping my eskrima, I steeled my nerves and reached for the doorknob. With one swift motion, I yanked the door and jumped out, pointing my eskrima like the deadly weapon it was. I've faced demons and vampires, but nothing could prepare me for the sight waiting for me outside my door.

There was a large, classic sleigh wedged in the snow that had accumulated outside of our apartment. It was bright red with ornate golden designs decorating it. It had two seats with a large cargo area, which was noticeably empty. Nearby, eight reindeer sputtered nervously as they idly wandered together in two rows. They were all hitched together, silver bells decorating their reins.

"No freaking way." I gasped.

As if on cue, someone pulled themselves out of a snow drift, muttering and cursing as he had been when I'd first heard the disturbance. He was a large man, and I mean a really large man. He was easily eight feet tall, with a glorious silver-white beard and a matching curlicue mustache. He wore a large, red-lined coat over a matching suit. He wore pristine black leather gloves and boots, and he looked thoroughly miffed.

"You're...you're..." I stuttered.

The man dusted himself off, shaking residual snow from his getup. "Of all the stupid, God-forsaken..."

That's when he finally seemed to notice me for the first time. He became perfectly still as he made eye contact with me. I stared back at him, still absolutely dumbfounded. We stood there, staring at each other like a couple of idiots in the snowy night.

The man seemed to regain his composure, straightening his coat and resting his hands on his rotund belly. "Well, Tobias Leight, it's nice to meet you."

"You know my name?" I said.

"You're..." I kept repeating.

The man seemed to regain his composure, straightening his coat and resting his hands on "Well of course, I'm—"

"Santa Claus." I said finally.

He waved his hands at me dismissively. "I've gone by many names, kid. Allfather, Father Christmas, Sinterklaas, Saint Nick. But you can call me Kringle, Kris Kringle."

"Kringle, huh?"

"In the flesh, for one night only." Kringle held his arms out grandly.

"And uh," I gestured to his sleigh and the reindeer. "I'm guessing those are yours?"

Kringle smiled proudly. "Sure are."

I narrowed my eyes. "But where's your hat, and your sack of gifts?"

Kringle cocked his head, wagging a finger. "And that's the thing. The whole reason I crashed in your front yard." He began. "While flying over the glorious city of Seattle, my sleigh was attacked."

"Attacked?" I asked. "Who attacks Santa's sleigh on Christmas Eve?"

I was still wrapping my head around the idea of there actually being a Santa Claus. Bloodthirsty vampires and ravenous demons, sure. But Santa Claus? This was just ridiculous.

"Imps." Kringle said simply. "Little scoundrels ambushed me on my way out of the city."

"Imps? What would imps what with your sack of presents?" I asked.

"The hat, don't forget the hat." Kringle added.

"Right." I said, a hint of skepticism in my voice.

"Hey, don't doubt the man in the red coat." Kringle waved his finger at me again.

"Sorry, I'm just having a hard time wrapping my head around this." I said, pacing in the snow. I'd put my eskrima away in the loose pocket of my pajama pants.

"What? You don't believe me?" Kringle said, perturbed.

"I just didn't think Santa Claus—"

"Kringle." He corrected.

"I just didn't think you were real." I said.

"Fine, go ahead. Ask me anything." Kringle challenged.

I took a moment to think about it. How could I test the guy and prove he was who he said he was?

"Okay, what did I want most for Christmas when I was nine?" I asked.

"Oh that's easy." Kringle waved dismissively at me. "You asked for a pet fire breathing dragon. For obvious reasons, I got you a toy dragon."

Damn, he was good. I remembered that toy dragon and the immense disappointment I felt that it could only shoot a plastic fire dart.

"Okay, so maybe you are San-I mean, Kringle." I said. "Back to my original question, then. What would imps want with your sack of presents? And your hat?" I made sure to mention his hat. He seemed pretty sensitive about it.

"Simple, really." Kringle began. "My hat and sack are my symbols of power. Think Poseidon's trident, or Tom Cruise's heels he wears in movies to look taller."

Okay, I liked this guy. His sense of humor was on point.

"Every year it's the same with the imps, usually I'm able to outmaneuver them. But they got lucky. And now they've made off with my stuff and are most likely on their way right now to take them back to their master."

I raised an eyebrow. "And who's their master?"

"Krampus, the Yule Devil." Kringle said. "He's a...rival of mine, sort of. He used to frighten children into behaving during the holiday season, but in recent years, he's gotten bolder. I fear he may be trying to sabotage me and Christmas in general."

"Why would he want to do that?" I asked.

"Krampus has gotten bitter as the years have gone by. Our very nature means he's constantly in my shadow." Kringle explained. "The people who still remember him see him as a devil, a force of evil that seeks to ruin Christmas time. I think he's decided to finally embrace that notion, and now he has my hat and sack. Without them, I won't be able to deliver gifts. No gifts, no Christmas time."

"Isn't the whole lesson in every Christmas movie is that it's not about the presents, but the time spent with your family and all that?" I asked.

Kringle scoffed. "Poppycock! Who doesn't love a good present?"

Fair enough. Who was I to argue with the big man himself?

"Okay, so what can I do to help?" I asked him.

Kringle raised an eyebrow. "You want to help me?"

I shrugged. "Of course, it's Christmas."

Kringle smiled. "Attaboy."

I ran back into the apartment. I quickly got myself dressed and prepared, making sure not to forget my charms bracelet or my spell-laden sheepskin jacket. It was going to be a cold, busy night. Once I was dressed and prepared, I came back outside.

"Okay, remind me of the plan." I asked.

"Krampus is most likely holed up in a place associated with evil and dark magic. Somewhere he'd find nice and cozy." Kringle explained. "You'll have to get there, find my stuff, and get out. Hopefully avoiding the imps, and Krampus himself. Trust me, you don't want to go up against that guy."

"You don't seem especially concerned about all of this." I noted. "Aren't you worried about Christmas?"

"Oh sure, but I have the best wizard for the job." Kringle winked, and I swear his eye twinkled.

I felt my face heat up at the sudden praise, but I shook it off. "Okay, and what do I do once I've got your hat and the sack of presents?"

"My hat has a jingle bell on it. Just give it a ring and I'll be right there." Kringle explained. "Any other questions?"

I thought about it for a moment. "In the song, Twelve Days of Christmas, why are so many of the presents birds?"

Chapter 7

Mr. Claus insisted he needed to stay with his sleigh. Something about keeping the reindeer in check and the Chicago Incident of '97. Who was I to question the great Saint Nick? Kringle had given me something to help me along in my search for Krampus. A single jingle bell. It was a simple silver bell. Real silver too, none of that cheap, chrome paint stuff. With it, I could create a link between it and the bell adorned on his cap. I stood outside our apartment complex, where a steady fall of snow had covered the streets. I used my eskrima to carve a small circle in the snow, placing the bell in the center. I placed a finger on the edge of the circle, and whispered a word. There was a barely audible snap as the circle locked into place and I began chanting nonsense syllables.

It was a simple tracking spell, something that just about anyone could pull off, even non-wizards. With a small effort of power, I willed the lone jingle bell to lead me to its brother. The jingle bell began to roll in the confines of the circle, leading north. Of course it was north, how appropriate. I smudged the circle with some snow and picked up the jingle bell, feeling the gentle tug urge me to get moving. The bell had a small tassel that I hung around my finger. The bell hung suspended at an angle as it guided me. I rubbed my hands together and breathed some hot air between them and began my trek. It was going to be a long night. I really wished I had a car, though with how heavy the snow was coming down, I would've been nervous to drive on the frost-slicked streets of Seattle.

I trekked through the snow for a good hour, and as I ventured into the night, I felt the pressure of the situation begin to bear down on me. It was up to me to save Christmas. On top of that, I still couldn't believe I'd met the real life Santa Claus. He was everything you'd expect, and more. He had the air of the holly jolly gift bringer you'd expect, but there was more to him. After all, he said one of his many names was Allfather. I tried not to think about the implications of that too deeply. There was too much to do.

That's when I started to recognize where I was. It was just over a year ago since I'd last been here. It was an old industrial park, warehouses were lined up in rows as far as the eye could see. But once I'd arrived, I knew exactly where I was headed. There was one warehouse in particular that not too long ago, had been used as a base of operations for a traitorous vampire scourge. It had since been abandoned and condemned. Even the city officials who had made the call weren't exactly sure why they had. But I knew why. It was a place of evil. It scared people. Mortals and non-mortals alike. Even though no one had been here in over a year, I could still feel the residual aura left behind by the previous occupants.

"That figures." I muttered, shivering.

I pocketed the jingle bell and took a quick look around the perimeter. It seemed all clear, but there was nothing to suggest that new tenants had moved in. I circled back to the front door and stared at it for a long moment, trying to steel my nerves. I made sure to have my lone eskrima in hand. Finally I puffed out a breath.

"Come on Tobias, get yourself together." I growled. "You've fought vampires, demons, and a fallen angel. What's one evil Santa reject?"

I huffed out a defiant breath and walked forward. There had been chains binding the front door shut, but surprisingly enough, they had been cut. Frost had coated the broken links. Well, wasn't that pleasantly ominous? I tugged the door open, disturbing the freshly fallen snow and headed inside. The lobby had been gutted. The receptionist's desk, benches, and decorative plants that had once filled the space were long gone, replaced with broken glass and dust. The doors leading into the warehouse proper were also gone, now there was only the dark void of the inner depths of the place.

I whispered a word and cast a night-vision cantrip. It allowed me to see a bit better in the dark without giving away my position with a light. I proceeded forward cautiously, trying not to let my imagination run wild with the insidious possibilities of what may lie in wait.

It wasn't long before I realized I definitely wasn't alone. My night-vision spell wasn't strong enough to fully reveal my surroundings, but I could see dark shapes moving through the place. They were small, weaselly things, not much bigger than a purse dog. They watched me from a distance, and as I delved deeper into the warehouse, they made themselves more obvious. They chittered and giggled, speaking in a language I'd never heard before.

Something clattered to the ground somewhere in the warehouse, echoing and making it impossible to tell where it came from. I spun around, trying to point my eskrima in every direction at once. That's when they struck. Something small but remarkably dense jumped on my back and knocked me to the floor. My eskrima clattered somewhere into the darkness. The creature on my back raked at me with its claws, but it wasn't smart enough to go for my head, and it struck uselessly against my back. I regained my senses and swung my elbow behind me. The creature shrieked and slid across the polished concrete floor. I scrambled to my feet and grabbed my eskrima where it had bumped into a metal shelf. I aimed it at the strange creature and even in the darkness of the warehouse, my night-vision cantrip revealed just enough detail to give me an idea as to what this thing was.

It reminded me of the classic gray alien you see in old movies and "leaked" tapes from Area 51. Its skin was coal black. Its head was bulbous and had eyes that were dark voids of nothingness that took up most of its head, making it hard to distinguish them from the rest of its body. Where its eyes ended, at the top of its head, curling ivory horns jutted out. Its limbs were skinny and attached to them were hands and feet just a little bit too large for its body. It had shining ivory claws and an oversized mouth of sharp teeth to match.

"Are you the head imp?" I asked nonchalantly.

The imp cocked its head at me, like a dog hearing a new sound.

"You know, how Santa has a head elf. His second in command, covers all the bases at the North Pole while the big man tries to repair his relationship with his estranged son? While also trying to find a Mrs. Claus before the de-Santafication process takes away his magic forever?"

The imp turned its head the other way. Clearly it had never engaged in banter.

"Oh come on. You haven't seen that movie? The Santa Clause 2?" I asked. "Come on, it's a classic."

The imp raised its head to the ceiling and let out a chittering cry. One by one, it's comrades in the shadows joined in, until a chorus of alien voices echoed all around me. It was a strange sensation, the noise reverberating to my very core.

"So you guys aren't fans of early 2000s Christmas movies." I sighed. "Shame."

I aimed my eskrima at the lone imp and shouted. "*Hinote!*"

The spell laid into my charms bracelet channeled into my eskrima and let loose a blazing cannonball at the imp. It exploded on contact and sent the imp flying. The horde of imps took that as their cue. Claws clacked against the concrete as the imps closed in and I quickly realized I was in deep reindeer shit. They emerged as a wave of darkness that my night-vision couldn't pierce.

"Oh crap! Oh crap!" I squealed as I turned to run the way I'd come. But as soon as I did, more imps rounded the corner. "Oh crap." I sighed as I slowed.

Imps came from every direction. They climbed over the shelving and scurried down the corridors. My head turned and swiveled in every direction as panic raced through me. In an act of desperation, I struck the ground with my eskrima and shouted, "*Kaze maximus!*"

Wind rushed out in all directions around me, creating a miniature tornado that grew and expanded in every direction. The flood imps were flung into the air, tumbling in all directions. The metal shelving creaked and groaned, before falling away and crashing into the next row. It created a domino effect. Shelves crashed into the next. Metal shrieked and twisted and the imps answered in kind as many of them were crushed by the metal. Several imps were impaled by the twisted metal of the destroyed shelving. Their wounds burst into flame instantly. They were weak to iron. Which meant, as ugly as these things were, the imps were fae. Iron was the bane of the fae, which meant I might have an edge on these things after all. My eskrima had an iron tip, but it wouldn't be enough.

While the imps were distracted, I quickly took stock of my surroundings until I found what I was looking for.

A crate that had been crushed in my giant domino display had been full of old rod iron poles. Perfect. I picked one up, testing its weight in my hand. Yeah, this would do nicely. There were a handful of remaining imps that had been spared from the carnage. And a sick sense of glee came over me as I approached the first.

The imp screeched and lunged for me. It was quick, but I had been ready for its reaction. I extended the iron pole towards it and the imp's expression turned to pure terror as it had no way of avoiding the pole. It impaled itself on my impromptu weapon, burning and wailing as the iron did its thing. I gave the pole a hard flick, the imp flying off of it, leaving behind a coating of smoldering, pale blood. I repeated the process again and again, a few imps got close to breaching my defenses, but I blew them away with wind magic before impaling them too. It wasn't long before I'd dispatched the remaining imps. They left behind a pile of burning corpses.

I wrinkled my nose. They stunk like burning pine and coal. They may be evil monsters, but at least they remained on brand, even in death. After my work was done, I tossed the bloodied pipe away, it clattered loudly on the ground, the sound reverberating throughout the empty warehouse.

"Pft, I don't see what the big deal is." I chuckled. "You guys couldn't rob a convenience store, let alone Santa's sleigh."

As if waiting for his moment, a hoof clopped on the concrete. Then a heavy snow boot. Chains clinked and clanked against each other as they dragged across the ground. The contradictory footprints continued until someone emerged from around the fallen metal shelving. The figure was hunched over, but was still a foot taller than Kringle. He wore a coat similar to Saint Nick's, but blood red and I caught the distinct smell of iron in the air. I had a feeling it wasn't from the iron rods or metal shelving. Two feet long curling ram's horns stuck out from his forehead, illuminated slightly by his glowing red eyes. Chains hung from his wrists and ankles, and to my surprise, he had two mismatched feet. One was a cloven goat's hoof, the other was more human and clad in a heavy snow boot. Long claws adorned each hand.

Ladies and gentlemen, Krampus had entered the building.

Chapter 8

"Little wizard," Krampus' voice echoed in my mind. "You have dispatched my underlings. Something that jolly old fool was never willing to do. I admire that tenacity, that fire in your heart."

Krampus extended a clawed hand to me. "Join me, and I can promise you will have everything you ever need. Money to thrive in this cursed, capitalist society. Power to protect those you love from those who would do them harm. You have gained many enemies, and more are to come if you continue down this path. But I can give you power. That of which rivals even the Fallen Son whose fate is so closely entwined with yours."

I could feel Krampus' presence in my mind. Urging me to take him up on his offer. It was a dark, cold power that coated my mind in dark permafrost.

Images of a carefree life as a servant of the dark Christmas spirit flashed through my mind. Offers of pleasurable company, money, and material things were whispered in my ears. A phantom sensation of colossal power tingled through my limbs. I could gain phenomenal cosmic power, all I had to do was sell my soul. I would be a liar if I said his offer wasn't tempting. But his offer wasn't one of sincerity but of convenience. If he pulled me under his influence, he wouldn't have to worry about the ass-kicking he was about to receive. A determined fire ignited in my heart. Krampus' dark influence retreated from my mind as the flames of will burned through me.

"You can take that offer and shove it up your half-goat ass." I spat.

I could feel Krampus' anger rise. And I could physically see it as frost formed on the ground at his feet and spread. I wasn't going to let this Christmas freak get away with this.

I raised my eskrima. "*Hinote!*"

White hot flames erupted forth and sped towards Krampus. The dark Christmas spirit extended his hand towards the flames. As he did, an arctic cold wind rushed past him and quickly snuffed out the flames, robbing them of their heat.

"Oh come on!" I growled. Again, I aimed my eskrima and shouted louder. "*Hinote!*"

Once more, flames rushed from my eskrima and barreled towards Krampus. But Krampus had not let up on his arctic winds, and the flames sputtered out before they could even get close. Then Krampus began to walk slowly towards me, the arctic winds never letting up. I held up my arms defensively over my face, trying to hide from the winds, but it was no use. The biting cold made my nose and fingertips ache with the beginnings of frostbite. Krampus seemed to be in no hurry.

"With you out of the way, that old fool will have no choice but to confront me himself." Krampus said. "Once I destroy him, Yule will be mine to rule. Humanity will worship me. They will write, sacrifice, and pray to me for their blessings and gifts. It will give me power, boy. First, the time of Yule, then for all of the year! For all time!"

I gritted my teeth and locked eyes with Krampus. "Dude, I can't even begin to tell you how much none of that is going to happen!"

I aimed my eskrima again, solidifying my will. My fire spell charm only had three charges, but with how angry and annoyed I was feeling, I didn't need it. "*Hinote!*"

Flames roared towards Krampus as if the arctic winds weren't even there. The flames struck the winter spirit. He roared and recoiled from the flames, stumbling back and shielding himself with his arms.

I panted. "Yeah, take that, you goat-dicked freak."

Krampus roared and thrust out a hand.

Frozen spears materialized in the air and flew towards me. I extended my hand and shouted *"Defendum!"*

A shield of pure kinetic force formed in front of me. Icicles shattered against it and littered the ground. I hadn't mastered the spell yet and it quickly fell apart. I felt lightheaded and fought to keep up straight. I was getting tired way too quickly. I had a feeling Krampus himself was to blame. The energy he radiated was dark and malicious and I could feel it nibbling away at my psyche. I cursed at myself. Why hadn't I woken Bishop up? Or even Scout? I'd been so excited to help Kringle out, that I had thrown rational thought to the wind. Now I was alone and clearly outmatched. I'd gotten one good hit in, but Krampus didn't seem even mildly inconvenienced. Krampus was a spirit as old as the tradition of Christmas itself, back when it had been known as Yule. He had over 1000 years of belief and fear put into his legend. That made a figure like him extremely powerful. He was practically a minor god. Sure his legends had faded into obscurity in the modern age, but he had plenty of credit built up. I decided to blame that on the crappy film from the mid-2010s, the one with evil cartoon gingerbread minions.

A hook attached to a chain dropped from his sleeve. Krampus began swinging it in a circle, building up momentum for his killing blow. I had to do something, and fast. I stumbled and as I caught my balance, something jingled in my pocket. I tapped my jeans and felt the familiar shape of the jingle bell that Kringle had loaned to me. An idea popped into my head. It was a long shot, but it was all I had left.

I took the bell out of my pocket and held it out towards the Yule Devil. The jingle bell may be a small little trinket, but I felt its immense well of power flood into me. Glowing blue-white light surged around me.

"No!" Krampus roared. "You fool! I'll kill you!"

I shook my head. "I don't think so! *Kōri!*"

Ice erupted from the ground and struck Krampus, piercing his chest. Krampus roared in pain, pulling himself off of the ice spike. He swung his hook at the ice and it shattered into a million pieces. I shuffled back a couple of steps, spun into a stance, jingle bell outstretched.

"*Kōri!*" Ice jutted out from all around Krampus and struck him all over. Slashing at his arms, piercing his legs, and striking his obscured face.

Krampus roared again, releasing a pulse of power. The ice shattered and Krampus swept his arm through the air. The ice coalesced into hundreds of frosty needles. He thrust his arm forward and the needles came racing towards me.

I raised the jingle bell into the air and shouted. "*Holi!*"

A cloud of green lights coalesced around me, and the needles evaporated into harmless snowflakes that tickled my skin.

"You toy with power you couldn't possibly understand, boy!" Krampus growled. "Give me the bell and I might just spare you yet."

"Do you really think I would agree to that?" I said in disbelief.

Krampus thrust his head forward and roared angrily. It was the first time I'd gotten a good look at him. He had all the worst features of a goat and a man combined. His eyes had the strange rectangular pupils of a goat with red irises. His jaw was partially extended with a large nose. Patchy fur covered his face with no rhyme or reason. He was scarred and mangled, the signs of someone who fought many battles and lived to tell the tale. Krampus was truly the stuff of nightmares.

"God damn, that's a face not even a mother could love!" I said.

"My mother left me at the top of the mountain to be sacrificed to wolves." Krampus retorted.

"Well that explains a lot. You've got mommy issues." I pointed out.

Krampus roared and lunged at me. I somersaulted forward as he flew over me. I aimed my eskrima and shouted. "*Kaze!*"

Wind rushed forth and knocked the Yule Devil prone. I rushed towards him, stuffing the bell and my eskrima into my pockets and hissed out another word of power and two of the rod iron poles scattered across the ground flew into my hands. With a yell, I thrust one through the palm of his hand. Krampus screeched in pain. I screamed in response as I stabbed the second rod through his other hand. Krampus screamed again.

I dug my hand in my pocket and thrust the jingle bell towards him. The right words seemed to just spill out of me. "Evil spirit of darkness and malice, I banish thee this night! Return to your domain of darkness and never return to terrify another child!"

Krampus screamed and writhed. "No! Nooo!"

The Yule Devil melted away into nothingness until I was standing over an empty coat. I nearly keeled over in exhaustion but I managed to stay upright. I huffed and puffed.

"Merry Christmas, bitch." I muttered.

I stepped over the coat and headed back towards where Krampus had first emerged. There was a small freestanding room that had once served as an office. And sure enough, inside was what I'd been tasked to find. Kringle's sack of presents sat in the corner, with his iconic hat sitting on top. With a grunt of effort, I pulled the sack over my shoulder. I put the cap on my head, and hoped Kringle wouldn't mind me stealing his look for a couple of minutes.

I made my way back outside into the cold and set the bag down on the ground. My back ached like a man three times my age. How did the jolly guy carry this around every year? I pulled the end of the hat around my shoulder. Sure enough, just like Kringle had said, there was a bell hanging from a string from the tip of the hat. It was nearly identical to the one Kringle had loaned to me. With a quick twitch of the wrist, I rang the bell. It jingled, and while it was a small sound, it echoed into the night. A subtle wave of magic went out into the world.

I waited, and for several long minutes nothing happened.

"Maybe this thing's busted." I said.

On cue, I heard the distant ringing of dozens of jingle bells. I looked up into the sky, and in the distance, I saw the man himself. Pulled by eight reindeer, Kringle's sleigh flew through the sky on a current of white light. He swooped past me overhead and made a U-turn as he began his descent. Using the road as a runway, Santa's sleigh landed and raced past me as it came to a stop. The big, burly man hoisted himself out of his sleigh. The reindeer sputtered and scratched their hooves against the snow-covered asphalt.

"Well done, Tobias Leight. You've saved Christmas." Kringle cheered. He clasped one hand on my shoulder and squeezed. "I knew I landed on the right wizard's front porch."

"Uh, thank you, Mr. Kringle." I said. I held out the loaned jingle bell to him. "I wouldn't have been able to do it without this."

Kringle held up his hand. "Keep it." He flicked his nose and winked. "You've earned it."

He let go of me and hoisted his sack over his shoulder. Kringle gave me a glance and smiled. "That's a good look on you."

I'd almost forgotten I'd been wearing his hat. Sheepishly, I pulled it off and handed it to him. "Sorry, hands were full."

"Not a problem, kid." Kringle assured me. "Anyone can wear the hat."

Kringle tugged the hat on with one hand. He turned and headed back to his sleigh. With more care than I would've expected, he tossed the sack into the trunk of his sleigh.

"You've done good work tonight, Tobias." Kringle smiled. "But I think I can take it from here."

"That's it?" I asked. "It's all good? Just like that?"

"Just like that, young man." Kringle nodded. "Christmas is a time for family, and the good men who stand between them and the encroaching darkness. Sometimes the conflict is nothing deeper than a good man standing against evil."

I blushed, not used to praise from someone as significant as Father Christmas. Kringle hopped into his sleigh and gave me a final salute. Then he whipped his reins, and the reindeer took off in a sprint. Before long, they defied all physics and lifted off into the night sky.

Kringle's voice echoed in the sky. "Merry Christmas to all! And to all, a good night!"

With a twinkle of light, the man himself was gone. I smiled up at the moon, where I'd last seen the holly jolly father of Christmas. Then as the task of heading home set in, I took a deep breath and started walking.

The next morning, I woke up sore and completely unrested. I hadn't gotten to sleep until late last night, or early in the morning depending on how you looked at it. The excitement of my adventure had kept me up for several hours longer than I had hoped. I lugged myself downstairs to find Bishop sipping on a cup of cocoa, reading a book as he always did.

He raised his mug to me. "Merry Christmas, Tobias."

"Merry Christmas, Bishop." I echoed. "You wouldn't believe the night I've had."

"Oh, I might have an idea." Bishop pointed with his mug.

Under the tree was a present I didn't recognize. My uncle and I had set up the presents the night before, so I knew what should be there. But something had made its way under the tree sometime during the night.

It was a tube wrapped in red wrapping paper decorated with little cartoon Santas. A bright red bow rested on the top. I raised an eyebrow as I walked over to it. Picking it up, something rattled inside.

"What is it?" I asked.

Bishop shrugged. "Open it."

I returned the shrug and started ripping the paper. It was a long cardboard tube with a fitted plastic cap. With a brief tug, I opened it up and looked inside. My eyes widened. I tipped the tube and held out my hand for its contents. A two-foot long length of wood slid out. It was carved with various runes that blended in well to the wood's texture. It was a short, wooden staff. It had a metal handle in the middle and a metal tip at each end. I spun it around in my hand, testing the weight. But as I did so, there was a subtle flash of energy, and the two-foot rod extended into a polearm about five feet in length.

"A new magic focus." Bishop beamed. "It looks good on you."

I grinned furiously as I twirled it around a couple of times. "Doesn't it?"

I looked inside the cardboard tube again and realized there was one more thing inside. I shook it out. It was a letter, rolled up and bound with a thin red ribbon. I slid off the ribbon and unfurled the parchment.

"Tobias,

Because of you, I was able to bring joy to the kids once again this year. Your bravery and determination were instrumental in my success this Christmas. I heard you lost one of your eskrima last year, and thought you might need a suitable replacement as you grow into the young wizard and protector of mortal kind you are. This polearm should serve you well. It can shrink into a more convenient size by giving it a spin. But be careful, I whacked myself in the face a few times while I was testing it out.

Merry Christmas,

Kringle

P.S. Be seeing you soon, kiddo. Hold on tight to that jingle bell. You never know when a little bit of Christmas magic could come in handy."

I smiled as I finished the letter and looked at Bishop. "Did you have something to do with all this?"

Bishop held up his hands, feigning innocence. "I didn't hear a dang thing until this morning. But it sounds like you did good work, as usual."

I looked up at the Christmas tree, the ornate star on top shining brilliantly. Sure, the world of magic and monsters could be a scary place. But it turned out there were some truly marvelous things still waiting in the wings.

I turned to my uncle. "Merry Christmas, Bishop."

Bishop winked. "And a Merry Christmas to you, Tobias Leight."

A Hunt with Bigfoot

It's Tobias' first day at his new day job, but it seems that a Celtic god has other plans for him. This story takes place six months after *Tobias Leight Saves Christmas*.

Chapter 9

My first shift at The Grind was not going well. Since I'd graduated from high school, I'd been focusing heavily on my wizard training. In many ways, it had paid off. But it hadn't paid well, in the literal sense. I was nearing the end of my apprenticeship and it had started making me stir crazy.

The first two hours of my shift had been a disaster, I'd managed to spill a bag of coffee beans, burn the coffee that had been roasting in the display window, and dropped a hot cup of coffee on my lap during my break. I was thoroughly peeved.

Something I had only learned fairly recently was that The Grind was a local hub for the supernatural community in Seattle, which partially explained why they were open at all hours, day and night. The place mainly catered to wizards, but there were plenty of supernatural creatures who frequented the place. I recognized several Blood Clan vampires, for example, but they weren't here to cause trouble.

The supernatural community of Seattle regarded The Grind as unofficial neutral territory. If you were a guest here, you agreed to play nice while on their property, no matter who you ran into. That wasn't much of an issue, anyways. I'd come to learn that many of the patrons were outsiders to their respective groups, in one way or another. Many of the wizards here were minor talents, those who were pretty much ignored by the Mystic Order. It was one of my many gripes with the wizard governing body. I picked out a few local fae as well, many of whom I'd come to know in my dealings in the city and the surrounding wooded areas.

The shift lead, and my trainer for the day, was a person named Remy. Remy was an interesting character. They were a young member of the Mystic Order, but like me, they tried their best to steer clear of them where they could. Remy used they/them pronouns, if I hadn't made that clear, and had a habit of shifting their form from male to female, and vice versa, depending on their mood that day. Currently, they were in their female body. They were of Hispanic origin, though I wasn't exactly sure from where. Nearly as tall as me, their shoulder-length brunette hair was put up into a ponytail. They had a streak of baby blue that lined the side of their head. They wore a white shirt and black jeans under a gray denim apron with many pockets and brown leather straps binding it to their body. It accentuated their curves in a way I admittedly found very distracting.

I'd had a crush on them ever since I'd started frequenting The Grind, but I was far too busy with my wizard training and duties to make a move. I wasn't shy or anything like that.

I was sitting in the small break room in the back, having freshly spilled my coffee all over myself. It consisted of a round folding table with four chairs and a counter with basic kitchen appliances, including a toaster and a microwave. A mini fridge sat in the corner, where employees could keep their drinks and lunches. Remy approached me while I dabbed at my soaked pants and shirt with a wash cloth. I wore a matching white shirt, so the coffee had done a thorough job of staining it. I grumbled angrily to myself, my skin still stinging where the hot coffee had soaked through.

"You alright, Tobias?" Remy asked, stifling a laugh.

"Don't patronize me." I muttered angrily, but I didn't mean it.

Remy smiled. "I was going to have another go at teaching you how to properly roast coffee, but you have a visitor."

"A visitor?" I eyed them.

Remy nodded. "Yep, asked for you personally." They hooked a thumb towards the front of the house. "Doesn't seem like someone you should keep waiting."

I frowned, wondering who it could be. It could've been a number of people, and none of them would be here with good news.

I sighed. "I'll be right there." I gestured vaguely to myself. "Sorta dealing with a crisis here."

This time, Remy made no effort to stifle a laugh. It was the kind of giddy laughter that shook their shoulders and squished their eyes shut. Damn, it was a cute laugh. With notable effort, I stopped myself from watching them too long and returned my focus to making myself at least semi-presentable to my mysterious visitor.

After a few more minutes of the futile effort, I finally gave up on salvaging the white shirt. The black jeans would survive, but the shirt would soon meet its fate in the trash can.

Truthfully, I wasn't too worried about meeting my visitor in coffee-stained clothes, I'd been stalling meeting whoever was waiting for me. Like I said, a mysterious visitor was almost never good news. Enough personal experience and TV dramas had proven that. I came out from behind the counter and into the coffee shop proper.

The Grind was a pretty cozy place, it's why I'd gravitated to it so hard before I even knew it was looped into the world of magic. Past the front counter was the sitting area. There were a few wooden café tables where patrons could sit, read, and type away on their laptops. But my favorite area was a bit farther back. Bookshelves with well-read books lined the walls, a standing lamp occupied each of the far corners. In the center were two couches on either side of a secondhand, wooden coffee table. Sitting on the couch facing the outer wall was a man I'd met once before, two years ago. The fact that he was here now did not bode well for my immediate future.

The man wore a maroon hoodie with a silver Celtic knot symbol on his right breast. His hoodie's zipper was down far enough to reveal he wore a forest green t-shirt underneath. He sure liked to stay on brand. He had long, rust red hair that was pulled back into a man bun, and a matching beard. He must've trimmed it recently, because it didn't cover his neck like the last time I'd seen him. He was nearly nine feet tall, and it made sitting on a normal human-sized couch awkward. His eyes were glowing faintly with a golden light.

I did my best to act casual. "Howdy, Lugh."

Lugh turned at the sound of my voice, and he gave me a pleasant smile. He was not what I pictured when I heard "Celtic God." Lugh was far more relaxed than any depiction of a pagan deity I'd read about or seen on tv. The god was sitting in the coffee shop as if he were a regular guy, sipping on a cup of coffee and reading a battered copy of "Of Mice and Men."

"Tobias, a pleasure." Lugh rose to meet me and held out his hand.

I took it, his grip was firm but gentle and I did my best to match it without giving away the fact that his presence here made me nervous as hell. He returned to his seat and I took the one across from him. I only now noticed that none of the other customers were milling about in this part of the shop. They all sat at the tables near the front, or took their coffee to go. I made note of several nervous glances. They might not know exactly who was sitting across from me, but they were smart enough to know they should probably steer clear.

"Uh Lugh, not that I'm not happy to see you, but what the hell brings you to town?" I asked him. "I haven't seen you since our last talk."

After I'd stopped a faerie queen's plans to create an army of uber vampires, Lugh had paid me a visit, and made me keenly aware that I hadn't seen the last of the faerie queen. My first guess was that the upcoming conflict he'd warned me about was on the horizon.

Lugh must've noticed my tense expression, and held up a placating hand.

"Not to worry, Tobias." Lugh said. "I'm not here on official business. I come for a personal favor."

That didn't ease my mind one bit. A god was asking me for a favor? There had to be a catch. My studies and training had taught me that much.

"What could I possibly do for a god?" I asked him.

Lugh's expression soured. He didn't like being called a god much. In truth, he was a member of the Tuatha Dé Danann, the progenitors of the sídhe and the rest of the fae. It made him an immensely powerful guy, and god just seemed like the right word to me. But Lugh didn't care to correct me.

"I have a friend who could use your help." Lugh began. "He lives in the forest nearby, and he's in danger."

I frowned. "And you need my help? Why can't you just help him yourself?"

Lugh sighed. "Being who I am, I'm not always free to act. There are rules that I can't really explain to a mortal, such as yourself."

I huffed out a breath.

Lugh shook his head. "I don't mean it as an insult, just a statement of fact."

"So what kind of trouble is your friend in?" I asked.

"There have been a string of killings in Mt. Rainer National Park." Lugh explained. "Mortal authorities are blaming it on a bear attack. But those clued in have their eyes set on my friend, who lives in the forest."

"So you want me to save your friend?" I asked.

"More like I want you to help him track down the real killer. And prevent those who hunt him from succeeding in their mission." Lugh said. "Are you familiar with the Aegis Institute?"

"Isn't that a shield from Greek mythology?" I asked.

"Yes, but not what I'm talking about." Lugh said. "The Aegis Institute is a mortal shadow organization that's clued into all things supernatural. They've taken it upon themselves to hunt magical creatures, collect magical artifacts, and prevent magical disasters."

"Take a shot every time you say 'magical.'" I chuckled.

"It's no laughing matter, Tobias." Lugh said gravely. "The Aegis Institute doesn't bother to differentiate between the good and the bad, if you belong to the supernatural world, they'll shoot first and ask questions later."

My face straightened. "Sounds like a bunch of douchebags."

Lugh nodded in agreement. "You'll have to track down the true killer before Aegis agents can sink their claws into my friend, and turn it in to them as proof. Otherwise, I fear my friend's people will see no choice but to go to war with humanity."

I frowned. "What? Can they not tell the difference between friend and foe either?"

Lugh sighed. "My friend and his people have not had the best of luck interacting with humanity ever since the white man colonized this continent."

I gulped. "I don't know if you've noticed, Lugh." I gestured to myself. "White guy. Are you so sure that your friend won't see me as an enemy as well?"

The god of justice chuckled. "I've already made him aware of you. He'll be expecting you. If you agree to help, that is."

I sighed. It wouldn't be wise to turn down Lugh. And he asked this of me as a personal favor, something the fae, let alone the Tuatha, wouldn't do lightly. Lugh was genuinely asking for my help, and I'd be a right bastard to turn him down.

"Just one thing, you wouldn't happen to have a car I can borrow?" I asked.

Chapter 10

As a matter of fact, the Celtic god of justice and light did not have a car I could borrow. The Williams family did, though. My relationship with the Williams family had grown distant in the last couple of years, ever since Claire had gone off to college. I didn't hear much from her, she rarely responded to my texts, let alone my calls. When she did text me back, the answers were short, quick and efficient, absent of the friendly banter we used to have.

But that was a problem for another day. Despite the distance that had formed between me and the Williams family, Mr. Williams still agreed to lend me his old Volkswagen Beetle. The car was not a pretty sight, and was one of Mr. Williams' handful of doomed restoration projects. It ran well enough, but the car was definitely not my type. And I didn't see myself driving it valiantly into battle in the future. Man, I needed my own ride. The nearly two hour drive in the dead of night did little to keep me entertained. The car was old enough that I didn't have a suitable contraption to hook up my phone for music, so I was left to the mercy of the radio. The drive was long, quiet, and lonely. I would have brought Scout to keep me company, but he and Bishop hadn't been home when I swung by to retrieve my gear.

But finally, I'd arrived. It wasn't hard to find a parking spot near the small office building that marked the entrance into the park. Lugh was a bit vague on the details on how I could find his friend once I was in the park. And by vague, I mean he offered no help on the subject. I cursed myself for not questioning Lugh more thoroughly.

I was wearing my sheepskin bomber jacket, which was magically enhanced with defensive spells, making it better than kevlar and a suit of armor combined wherever it covered. Plus, it kept me warm and cozy even in the coldest Washington weather. It was summertime, which took most of the bite out of the cold night, but I was still thankful to have it.

Dangling from my wrist was my charms bracelet, a specialized magic focus that helped me with specific spells I sucked at, namely of the stealth and fire kind. The latter of which I didn't plan to use if I could avoid it, I didn't need to start a forest fire today. At least, I hoped not. Finally, I had my polearm, a two-foot long wooden rod that could extend into a five foot long martial staff with a flick of my wrist. It had an iron grip in the center with two matching tips on either end. I wore a magnetic baldric underneath my jacket, which kept the polearm attached to my back. It rested just within my reach for easy access.

I hauled a backpack out of the car's passenger side, which I'd packed with a bit of food and water, as well as a spare change of clothes. I didn't think this ordeal would take too long, but I wanted to be prepared. I wasn't sure exactly what waited for me in these woods. I locked the car and started walking. TV and movies don't really give you a good idea of just how dark it can get in the middle of nowhere. With no city lights to keep the darkness at bay, I was at the moon's mercy. I could barely see two feet in front of me. I muttered a simple spell and the world became a bit more clear with the help of my night vision cantrip.

Without the spell, I'd probably have fallen on my ass a dozen times or more. I hadn't wasted any time trekking off the hiking trail. There were plenty of tree roots and rocks that would've tripped me with no remorse, and I took careful steps to avoid them. I hummed the *Lost Woods* theme from *Ocarina of Time* as I wandered in the woods for nearly an hour and I was starting to feel like an idiot. I had no idea who or what I was supposed to be looking for. I had half a mind to turn back, when something made the hairs on my arm stand on end.

I reached back and hovered my hand over my polearm, staying as still as I could. My eyes darted back and forth, looking for whatever had set my instincts on high alert. A roar pierced the night, visibly shaking the leaves overhead. The sound was alarmingly reminiscent of a bear, and for all my magical abilities, I was not looking forward to a bear encounter.

Another moment passed and I very quickly changed my mind. I would've much rather taken on a bear. A giant...thing leaped through the air towards me from somewhere above. It was completely obscured in shadow, but I vaguely recognized the shape of a very large, very angry man-shaped thing. Its eyes glowing red with malice. The beast landed and I backpedaled as I pulled my polearm over my shoulder and in front of me in a defensive position. The ground shook as the creature landed, kicking up dirt and debris in every direction. I shielded my eyes as I prepared a spell. Screw worrying about a forest fire, I was not dying tonight.

I extended my arm, aiming my polearm at the creature. I channeled my magic through my charms bracelet as I called up fire. "*Hinote!*"

A bowling ball-sized comet of fire exploded outwards and flew towards the mysterious monster. The thing extended a ginormous hand towards the incoming fireball. Imagine my surprise when my flames melted into green streams of light and simply dissipated into the forest. Before I could ready another strike, the thing let out an ursine roar and leaped toward me. I let out a high pitched yelp. A creature of that size had no business moving that fast.

Before I could let loose with another blast of fire, the monster was on top of me. It knocked me to the ground, tossing my staff away and pinning me. It roared in my face, giving me a good whiff of its stank breath. The roar stopped abruptly and large round eyes examined me up close and personal. It gave my hair a sniff and then cocked its head like a confused dog.

"Druid?" The beast spoke in a deep, gravelly voice.

For a moment, I didn't dare speak. But then I managed to say, "Uh, wizard, actually."

"You are the one Lugh sent?" The beast asked.

I was doing my best to remain calm and rationalize the fact I was talking to some monster of the forest. "Yeah, that's me. Uh, my name is Tobias Leight. And you are?"

The beast let me up, taking a few steps back to give me some space. It stepped into a shaft of moonlight, and I got my first good look at the creature. It was ten feet tall, and nearly half as wide. The creature's body was composed of dense muscle, covered in well groomed brown fur, save for its chest, face, hands, and feet, where its thick skin was black as coal. The fur growing from its head hung in a thick, frizzy mess. Its face reminded me of a bulldog, wrinkled with an underbite and pronounced eyebrow ridges. Its eyes were large, brown discs that twinkled with human-like intelligence.

"You may call me 'He Who Walks Among the Oaks and Listens to their Whispers', it is nice to meet you." The beast said. "My apologies, I did not realize who you were. When you attacked, I thought you may be with the ones who are hunting me."

"He Who Walks Among the Oaks and Lis—?" I stuttered. "I think I'm gonna call you Oak, if it's alright with you?"

He Who Walks Among the Oaks and Listens to their Whispers seemed to contemplate this for a moment, then nodded. "Oak will do. But please refrain from using fire magic while in my woods. I just redecorated."

I chuckled at the comment, though I couldn't tell if he'd meant it as a lighthearted warning or not.

Nervously, I cleared my throat and said, "Okay Oak, I guess we should have a chat."

Lugh could have freaking told me that his "friend" in the forest was an actual, honest-to-God Bigfoot, but I'd have that discussion later. It made sense why these Aegis Institute people were hunting him now. If I didn't know any better, and thought I did, I'd have pegged him for the recent killings too.

Oak and I sat in a small clearing in the woods. The sasquatch was seated on a fallen tree, while I'd found a comfy rock to use as a stool. The forest giant had gathered some tinder and lit it aflame with some of the most effortless magic I'd ever seen. We sat huddled around the fire, and I realized it was probably more for my benefit than his. His thick pelt probably kept him plenty warm in the frigid night.

"I have to ask, how do you do that?" I began.

"Do what?" Oak asked innocently.

"Your magic," I answered. "I've never seen someone melt a spell as effortlessly as you did. Not to mention the campfire, you barely twitched a finger."

"Ah, right," Oak said. He examined his hand for a moment, as if pondering the idea himself. "Magic is to my kind as breathing is to you. It is just part of who we are. My forefathers were the ones to teach it to the native tribes before the white man came along."

I snuffed the urge to apologize for something that had happened a couple hundred years ago that I had nothing to do with. "Erm, right."

"I trust that Lugh has informed you of my plight?" Oak asked. I was glad for the change of subject.

"Something about supernatural killings in the forest. These Aegis Institute twats seem to want to pin the blame on you." I summarized.

Oak nodded, it threw me off how strange such a simple movement looked on the giant. "Yes, I have remained hidden from them for now." Oak said. "But it will not be long before they are able to track me down. They may be made up mostly of regular folk, but the Aegis Institute has gathered a vast network of resources over the years. They have access to magic that even your Mystic Order deems inappropriate."

Yeesh, that was saying something.

"Okay, so what do we do?" I asked.

Oak held up his hands. "That is what you are here for, wizard. You tell me."

My face twisted up as I tried to think things through. The answer was pretty obvious, honestly. It was just going to be damned annoying to pull off.

"So we find the real killer?" I hypothesized. "And...what? Turn them in to the Aegis Institute?"

"Find the real killer, that I can agree on. He must be brought to justice." Oak said. "But I am not so sure that turning them over to a mortal shadow organization would be the right move."

I puffed my cheeks. "Well, when you say it out loud like that, it sounds stupid."

"That is because it is stupid," Oak said matter-of-factly. I didn't get the impression that he was trying to be rude or anything, but it stung anyway. "Man acts recklessly when confronted with things they do not understand."

I was starting to debate whether or not I cared much for He Who Walks Among the Oaks and Listens to their Whispers. Oh, who was I kidding? Oak was the chillest sasquatch I'd ever met. Granted, the sample size was very small, but hey, who was counting?

"Any chance we'd be able to scare off these Aegis jerks?" I asked.

Oak shrugged his massive shoulders. "Probably not. Most likely, it would only encourage them to stick their nose where it does not belong. But first, we will have to find the true culprit."

Chapter 11

Oak and I delved deeper into the woods. For such a big guy, Oak moved through the woods as silent as a cat. I barely noticed the sound or rumble of his footsteps. Combined with his magic, it was no surprise to me that Bigfoot had yet to be found. I couldn't even imagine He Who Walks Among the Oaks and Listens to their Whispers or his kin spending their days in a zoo exhibit. The gentle giant of the forest radiated power and intelligence that I'd seen only a couple of other times in my experience with the paranormal. But he was the first "good guy" I'd met who possessed it.

While Oak moved swiftly and without a sound, I stumbled over every third rock and snapped every twig in my path trying to keep up with the big guy. We wouldn't be sneaking up on anyone with my clumsy ass following the forest giant. I was about to suggest we take a short break to orient myself, when Oak stopped dead in his tracks. A wave of sickly energy hit me a moment later, the hairs on my neck stood on end. I pulled my polearm from over my shoulder and shifted my stance. Something was stalking us and it was giving off some serious power.

"Oak—?" I began to whisper.

The big guy raised a hand, urging me to be quiet. Oak was stone still, not daring to move a single inch. Whatever was watching us, it was clearly nasty enough to give Oak pause. Oak's fur began to bristle, like a cat trying to appear bigger than it was when it encountered a predator or rival.

"Reveal yourself, *yee naaldlooshi*." Oak rumbled.

"Yehnul-what?" I said, struggling to repeat what the giant had said.

"Skinwalker." Oak said simply, not taking his eyes off of a large bush fifty feet away.

As if on cue, something emerged from the brush. It was a large beast, and didn't quite match anything else in the animal kingdom. It had the basic build of a coyote, but four times the size. Its fur was patchy and half a dozen different colors common for canines. Its snout and face were covered in reptilian scales, instead of fur. Its upper legs were covered in dark feathers, and instead of paws, it had large, clawed crow's feet. Its eyes burned with an angry red light.

"So, not friendly." I noted.

"Beast of the Forest." The creature's voice slithered out, completely out of sync with its mouth. It turned its attention to me. "And a practitioner of the arts. Interesting."

"And what are you supposed to be?" I asked.

The creature seemed to smirk. Then, in the blink of an eye, the creature changed. Where the strange creature feature stood a moment ago, there was now a man. Even in the darkness, I could tell he was of Native American descent. His long, straight black hair went past his shoulders, He had high cheekbones and a gaunt face. He was skinny, but not malnourished. He wore an animal pelt over his shoulders and denim shorts that had probably been pants at one point, but they'd been ripped off below the knee.

"Sheesh, buddy you are one fucked up Animorph." I said, my mouth failing to consult my brain before spitting out the words.

The man arched his brow.

"I mean seriously, I've read those books and they've got some messed up stuff." I rambled. "But you take the cake by far."

The skinwalker turned his attention from me to Oak. "Forest Dweller, does the mageling speak for you?"

"I speak for myself, skinwalker." Oak's voice rumbled. "What is your name? And what is your purpose here?"

The man smirked. "I have gone by many names over the years." He paused as he seemed to consider his thoughts. "But you may call me Hok'ee."

For a second, I thought he said his name was "Hawk Lee", which would've been pretty cool, admittedly. But I vaguely recognized the emphasis and pronunciation he used, it was definitely Native.

"You're...what? Nisqually? Makah, maybe?" I guessed, though my familiarity with Native tribes was limited. Curse the public school education system.

"Navajo, actually." Hok'ee corrected. "At least I was, long, long ago."

I snapped my fingers. "Right, skinwalkers are a Navajo thing."

Hok'ee smiled amusedly. "My kind have many names. But yes, I am what the Navajo and modern social media would call a 'skinwalker.'"

"So that IS you in all those goofy TikTok videos." I said.

"Tick tock? I don't see how a clock is relevant here." Hok'ee said, genuinely confused.

"Not what I—never mind, forget it." I grumbled.

The sasquatch turned his gaze to Hok'ee. "You are far from home, are you not? A strange coincidence, given the rise of deaths in these woods."

Hok'ee smiled. He looked far too comfortable for a guy facing off against a wizard and a Bigfoot in the dead of night. My grip tightened on my polearm. Usually I liked a bad guy who was down for some less-than-witty banter, but something about this guy made my skin crawl.

"You're smart, for a great big ape." Hok'ee said, a mocking tone to his voice.

"I thought Native Americans were supposed to respect nature?" I said, gesturing to Oak. "Seems like you and Yogi here should be good buddies. Although he might be more of a Baloo. No wait, Baloo lives in the jungle. That never made sense to me. Since when do bears live in the jungle?"

"He is a skinwalker, Tobias." Oak's voice rumbled. "A bastardization of everything the Navajo, and all Native tribes for that matter, hold dear."

I narrowed my eyes at Hok'ee. "So you're not even going to try and hide the fact that you're behind the forest killings? Why?"

"I have my reasonings, child of the white man," Hok'ee said. "The sacrifices I've made so far fuel my power. They make me stronger. Not to mention, they are a signal fire to my brethren. I plan to form a new nation of skinwalkers. We will call Mt. Rainier our home."

"If you think I will allow that," Oak took a step forward, shaking the trees around him. "then you are more foolish than I realized. You have already trespassed in my home. Then you go about killing mortals for your own selfish gain."

"And to top it off, you've brought these Aegis Institute guys down on my friend here." I said, twitching my polearm in Oak's direction.

"Well, I didn't want to risk a fight with one of the ancient people of the forest. I thought it was better left to the professionals." Hok'ee admitted. He cocked his head, as if listening for something. "Well, would ya look at that? Right on time."

Hok'ee stood there one second, and the next, he was replaced by a monstrous hawk. His voice echoed in my mind. "*It was nice to meet you both.*" Then he took off into the night sky.

"No!" Oak growled. "We must go after him!"

"Wait a second, Oak." I said, my eyes darting back and forth as I tried to look everywhere all at once. "We have more company."

No sooner had I said it, we were surrounded. Men in black surrounded us, wielding automatic weapons with mounted flashlights. They all barked orders and took ready positions around us.

"Put the stick down and get on your knees! Both of you!" A voice spoke up.

"You've got to be kidding me." I muttered.

There were nearly a dozen agents, all fitted out with tactical gear well suited for a midnight hunt in the forest. The light from their mounted flashlights made my night vision cantrip useless, but I didn't turn it off. I had a feeling I'd need it again before long.

"I said put the weapon down and get down on the ground!" The agent said again.

"Oooh, aren't you guys from the X-Files? Where's Mulder and Scully?" I asked, taking a more casual stance. "We haven't met yet. My name is To—"

"Tobias Leight. Wizard. Resident of Seattle." The agent said.

Okay, so they knew who I was. That was only mildly concerning. "And you are?"

The agent who had been speaking lowered his weapon and took a couple steps forward. He clicked a button on his helmet, and his night vision visor rose from his eyes. He was a white guy, typical for a douchebag secret government agent. I couldn't tell much about him with all of that gear he had on, except for a pair of cold, gray eyes.

"Agent Charles Bardot. You're interfering with official Aegis business, wizard." He said.

So these guys were with the mysterious Aegis Institute. But I held out hope that they could introduce me to David Duchovny and Gillian Anderson.

"And what business would that be?"

Bardot flicked his head towards Oak. "Your big friend there. He's responsible for numerous killings in the park. It's my job to bring him in. Hot or cold, it doesn't matter."

I sidestepped into a battle-ready stance, raising my polearm. "You've got the wrong guy. And trust me, you guys don't want this fight."

Point of fact, I didn't want this fight either. Wizard or not, having a dozen guns trained on me did not bode well. But I wasn't going to let these guys lay a finger on Oak. Not while the real killer was still at large.

"Ready for a fight, big guy?" I asked.

Oak said nothing. I looked to where he'd been standing a moment before. The Bigfoot was nowhere to be seen. My eyes widened as I realized I was now alone with the trained gunmen.

"Thanks for the heads up." I sighed.

I doubted I could take on this many gunmen by myself, but I didn't plan to. It was time to make like a tree and catch up with the runaway Bigfoot.

I closed my eyes and took a deep breath. I extended one hand forward, my fingers loose. "*Moya.*"

Mist coalesced all around me and my surroundings, thickening until I couldn't see a foot in front of me. The Aegis agents started panicking and shouting. I could see the dim glow of their flashlights zipping back and forth in the thick mist. I wasted no time in hauling ass out of there. Several shots went off, one hitting me in the back. I grunted as the strike nearly knocked the wind out of me, but I kept running.

"Hold your fire!" Bardot's voice called out.

By the time they'd gathered their wits and my mist dissipated, I'd be long gone. Now I just had to track down my sasquatch buddy so we could find the real killer. I tried to rack my brain on anything I knew about skinwalkers, but I was flooded with adrenaline and only focused on getting to safety.

After several minutes of running, I stopped to rest. I put my hand against a tree and doubled over as I tried to catch my breath and process everything that was going on. I had a feeling that Hok'ee the

Skinwalker was very dangerous. Not because he was extremely powerful, though I suspected he was. He was smart enough not to take on He Who Walks Among the Oaks and Listens to their Whispers head on, instead he suckered a mortal shadow organization into doing it for him. And to kill two birds with one stone, the murders that he was using to bait Aegis was also fueling his power. I had to assume he was as powerful and as smart as he came off, otherwise I had no chance of beating him. I considered calling my uncle Bishop to assist. A quick glance at my phone showed that was not an option.

"No signal, typical." I sighed, holding my phone over my head. "3G, 4G, 5G, all these Gs and I can't even get a single bar."

"Clever trick, getting away from those men." A familiar voice said.

I followed the voice up into the trees, where I saw the dark shape of Oak hanging from a branch that probably shouldn't have been able to hold his weight.

"Yeah, no thanks to you." I said, a hint of bitterness tinging my words.

"My apologies, wizard." Oak hopped down from his perch and landed a few feet away. His landing made barely a sound and didn't even shake the ground around him.

I considered that for a moment. "Stealth magic, that's how your kind has remained hidden."

"Very good." Oak nodded.

"Didn't really pick up on it until your disappearing act back there." I said. "Pretty nifty trick for a big guy."

"I could say the same to you." Oak said. "Using the cold mountain air to assist in your mist spell was wise."

"Thanks." I beamed, as if I had known it would've worked out that way. The mist spell was a riff on a smokescreen spell I'd been working on but had yet to perfect. "So what now? Any ideas on how to find Hok'ee?"

Oak nodded and then extended a pointed hand deeper into the forest. "The skinwalker will be at the heart of the forest, where most men do not dare to travel."

"Sounds good to me. Let's take a walk in the woods, then."

Chapter 12

The forest was eerily silent. Save for my clumsy footsteps. He Who Walks Among the Oaks and Listens to their Whispers' large feet didn't make a sound, in spite of me. We were trekking downhill, over gnarled roots and dead leaves.

"Hey, this is a big forest." I pointed out.

"An astute observation." Oak said. Even though it was dark, I knew he was smiling from the tone of his voice.

"But I haven't seen a single animal around." I continued. "I haven't heard a single cricket."

"Ah, so that is what you mean." Oak rumbled. "Blame the skinwalker. The stink of his magic and his soul scare all the critters away. You would be hard-pressed to find even a grizzly milling about."

That made sense, from what I'd been learning over the last couple of years. The supernatural had a way of scaring off wildlife. The animals might not know what it is that was freaking them out, but they were smart enough to steer clear and keep quiet. They were certainly smarter than me. With my polearm gripped tight in between my hands and a sasquatch at my side, we delved deeper into the forest.

After twenty minutes of walking, we'd reached the bottom of the hill. As soon as I stepped into the valley, a pungent odor assaulted my nose.. I covered my nose with my sleeve as I slowed to a stop.

"Gah, what is that?" I groaned.

Oak's nostrils flared. "Dark magic, and the death that is empowering it."

A sickly green light lit up somewhere deep in the forest. The trees cast long, strange shadows all around us. I covered my eyes as best as I could, trying to see through the blinding light.

"The fiend." Oak growled.

"What's he doing?" I whispered.

"He is using the energy from all the death and chaos he's caused." Oak said. "He means to channel all that energy into himself."

"And if he succeeds?" I asked.

"I suspect he will become something of a demigod," Oak rumbled. "With that much power, he will be able to gain the followers he so desperately craves. It would not take long for the state of Washington to have quite the skinwalker problem."

"A cult of skinwalkers in my backyard? That's not gonna fly." I said. "Come on. Let's go ruin his night."

I took a step forward, but a great big hand gripped my shoulder. I looked up to see Oak with a serious expression on his face.

"You cannot fight him, wizard." He said.

"Why not?" I asked.

"You are young, only just now coming into your power." Oak said. "He would kill you."

I shook my head. "Come on big guy, can't you root for the underdog? Either way, I can't let him eat up a bunch of death juice and turn into a super-powered Charles Manson. I have to try."

Oak looked towards the light, the gears turning in his head. Then he looked back to me. "Very well, you get his attention. I will join you shortly."

Oak braced himself before leaping into the air. He hung from a tall tree before leaping to the next. Before long, he faded into the foliage and seemed to disappear. I watched him go, considering what I'd seen for a moment.

"Man, I've gotta get him to teach me that." I said. I refocused my attention on the strange green light. Steeling my nerves, I walked towards it.

As I got closer, the green light gave way to what I realized must've been Hok'ee's camp. There was a basic tent nearby, made of animal skins propped up with large branches. There were several logs bordering the campsite in a twelve-foot-wide circle. In the center was the source of the green glow, a bonfire with flames reaching eight feet into the air. The flames had a strange quality to them I couldn't quite pin down. They were the same sickly green color and there seemed to be...things moving around in the flames. Every few seconds, I saw a distorted face float from one edge of the flames to the other. There were voices coming from the bonfire as well, but they were too faint and garbled for me to make sense of them. Wisps of flame broke off and seemed to float independently for a few moments before fading away.

"Burning Man, eat your heart out." I said to no one in particular.

Hok'ee casually emerged from behind the ethereal flames, as if he wasn't preparing a dark ritual. I couldn't quite put my finger on it, but he was different somehow. He was somehow...more. The way he moved was less than human, it was too smooth, too precise, absent of any clumsy imperfections.

"Thank you for coming, wizard." Hok'ee said. "I must admit, I like the idea of an audience being present for my ascension."

"What can I say? It's not everyday you get to mess up a skinwalker's creepy death magic ritual." I said.

Hok'ee smiled. His teeth had all been filed to jagged points. "You can't stop what's happening here, wizard. The ritual has already begun. Even now, the spirits of the fallen flow into me."

"Gross." I said. "Listen guy, I'm going to give you one chance to stop the ritual. Otherwise I'm going to have to lay a major beatdown on ya."

"Please, wizard. You are simply not strong enough to challenge me." Hok'ee said matter-of-factly. "Either way, the ritual has already begun. It cannot be stopped."

"Dude, I tackled a sídhe queen and lived to tell the tale. If you think you scare me, you've got another thing coming." I pointed my polearm at him. "Last chance, step away from the creepy ritual fire."

"Like I said, the ritual has already begun." Hok'ee said, exasperated. "Even if I wanted to stop the ritual, it can't be done."

"Don't say I didn't warn you." I sighed. I spun my polearm once and took aim. "*Kaze!*"

A column of wind erupted forth, rushing towards the skinwalker. The skinwalker leaped to the side as he melted into his mismatched, bestial form. Hok'ee flanked me, running along the border of his camp and heading straight for me. I pivoted, spinning my polearm as I did. I hadn't let up on my wind spell, so wind rushed all around me in every direction until I lined it up with the skinwalker. I grunted as I renewed the spell, and a renewed blast of wind headed straight for the skinwalker. But the skinwalker was too fast and nimble. Before my spell reached him, he jumped into the air, leaping straight for me.

The skinwalker hit me hard, throwing me to the ground and pinning me there. He struck at me with his fangs, and it was pure luck that I was able to dodge each strike. I struggled to free myself from under Hok'ee, but it was no good. He was far too strong and too heavy. I needed to get him off me and fast. I hadn't wanted to resort to fire magic while in the forest, but I was desperate.

"*Hinote!*" I yelled defiantly. I was able to move my arm just enough to aim my hand at him. A gout of flame belched outward and struck the beast in its chest.

Hok'ee yelped like a dog in pain before backpedaling away. It was a strange thing to see from a quadruped, but I didn't have time to dwell on it. I hissed out a word, and a small but powerful gust brought my polearm back into my hands. Hok'ee didn't stay on the retreat for long, rushing me again. I spun my staff and struck him in his snout. He yelped again but wasn't deterred, snapping his jaws at me. His fangs found purchase and sunk into my forearm. I cried out in pain, and retaliated with an elbow from my free arm, followed up by a knee to his jaw. Hok'ee growled in pain and flung me away towards the ghastly bonfire. I tumbled across the ground, but managed to recover into a three-point crouch.

I got lucky using fire the first time. Oak had been there to dispel the flames. But this time, the sasquatch wasn't available to stop the consequences of my actions. The flames from the spell had hit their mark, but they'd also bled past the skinwalker and caught the brush nearby. With all of the excess brush and debris laying around the forest floor, it didn't take long for a simple fire blast to engulf the surrounding area and erupt into a full on forest fire.

The flames robbed the air of moisture, making each breath I took harsh and ragged. Embers bit at my exposed skin and spread amongst the brush. Soon the nearby trees had been engulfed by the flames as well. Lesson learned, don't use freaking fire magic in the forest. Hopefully Oak would be able to help me quell the flames. But that would have to wait until I'd dealt with Hok'ee.

I examined my arm for injuries. Hok'ee hadn't been able to break through the spell-woven fabric of my jacket, but my arm still hurt like hell. At the very least, there'd be a nasty bruise. I spun my polearm, ending in a defensive stance with the polearm stretching across my body. I needed a way to pin this guy down, and fast. I wouldn't survive much longer in a straight-up fight.

"You are strong for your age, wizard." Hok'ee's voice slipped from between his maw as he waded through the flames. "Submit to me, become one of my followers, and I promise you will know power beyond your wildest imagination."

"You already know I'm not going to take that offer, right?" I retorted.

Hok'ee shrugged, a strange movement for his beast form. "It was worth trying. Fear not, wizard. I will remember your valiant effort long after I've killed you."

While he spoke, I had been preparing a spell. Something new I had been working on. Fire had always been tough for me to conjure without the help of my charms bracelet. I'd only ever been able to call it up in acts of desperation. And even then, I didn't have much control of the flames. So instead, I'd been working on mastering its opposite. It was a work in progress, but it might just be able to save me here.

I spun my polearm, gathering whatever moisture remained in the tree roots underground. "*Mizu!*"

Water coalesced in the the air and formed itself into a ball six feet in diameter. I breathed heavily, the effort of gathering and maintaining the water had taken up a great deal of my reserves, especially amidst a forest fire. I thrust my polearm forward, the sphere of water bursting forward and dousing the skinwalker before he could react.

I pulled my polearm back towards my body. "*Págos!*"

I robbed the skinwalker and the water that drenched him of as much heat as I could. In less than a second, the water froze and formed two inch thick icy bindings around his extremities, pinning him where he stood. The rest of his body was covered in a thick layer of frost. I doubled over, the effort draining me significantly. But for the moment, the skinwalker was unable to move. It wouldn't last long. The raging forest fire was already weakening the icy prison. I could see water droplets trailing down his body.

Hok'ee spoke, despite being half frozen. "Surely you know that this won't hold me for long, mageling."

"Don't need it to." I panted, forcing myself to stand straight. "Just long enough for my big, furry friend to disrupt your ritual." I hooked a thumb back towards the ritual site where the ethereal flames danced and mingled with the regular inferno.

Hok'ee's eyes widened in alarm and I turned to meet my sasquatch buddy. He Who Walks Among the Oaks and Listens to their Whispers had made his move shortly after I'd engaged the skinwalker in battle. He stood over the green flames, performing a strange dance of some sort. His arms moved in slow, circular motions while his fingers moved in a much faster, more articulate way. I winced when I noticed the singed fur near his hands and feet. Oak had gotten caught in the literal crossfire and a pang of guilt pierced my chest. Bands of light emanated from his body, piercing the flames as he worked.

"No!" Hok'ee cursed. "I will not allow this!"

I heard the ice crack and I turned back to the skinwalker, aiming my polearm. "*Págos!*" A fresh layer of ice and frost formed over the skinwalker, repairing the damage he'd done to his bindings.

"Anytime now, Oak!" I shouted over my shoulder. "I can't hold this fucker forever!"

Oak gave me a disapproving glance before returning his focus to the spellwork. The ice was already melting, sharp cracks forming near the skinwalker's limbs. Hok'ee shuddered. I kept my polearm aimed at him. He was about six feet away. At the speed I'd seen him move, if he were to break free, I'd have less than a second to react. Shards of ice fell away as the skinwalker freed one of his forelegs.

"Oak!" I shouted urgently.

"Patience, wizard." Oak said way too calmly. "This takes time."

"I don't think he cares!" I growled back.

One of Hok'ee's back legs jerked free of the ice, giving him more leverage to struggle. He began to flex his body, straining back and forth in an attempt to break the ice completely. At this rate, I only had a few seconds before he broke free. And I was already running on fumes.

"Just a few more seconds..." Oak mumbled absentmindedly.

All at once, Hok'ee's icy bonds shattered. The skinwalker rushed forward without wasting a second, sprinting towards me with his fangs bared. I yelped as I took a step back, holding my polearm up defensively.

The mutant canine tackled me, jaws locking around my polearm as he took me to the ground. I felt the top of my head get hot as the flames crept closer. But it was all I could do to keep the skinwalker from tearing my throat out.

The skinwalker snarled and tried his damnedest to rip my polearm away. His bird-like talons ripped and tore at me, but the awkward positioning prevented him from striking any of my vulnerable bits. His talons raked uselessly against my jacket, the spells that my uncle had woven into them being the only reason my guts hadn't been spilled everywhere.

It wouldn't take long for my jacket to slip or for the skinwalker to get lucky. Sooner or later, his savage talons would hit their mark and I'd be in serious trouble. I tried to raise my arms so I could throw him off with a wind spell, but he was too fast and strong. With every attempt, Hok'ee swiped my arms away. I continued to struggle, but it didn't do much but annoy him.

The skinwalker stopped suddenly, locking his eyes on the ritual flames. There was a shudder of magical energies through the air. Hok'ee snarled and leapt off of me, towards the flames. I rolled over, my body sore from the beating I just took. My jacket could deflect blades, bullets, and spells, but the kinetic energy still bled through. Which meant I'd be sporting a giant bruise or two across my torso.

The magical flames were writhing, as if they were agonized by Oak's disassembling. Speaking of Oak, the big guy was dancing circles around the ritual flames as Hok'ee slashed at him with his fangs and talon. It was strange to watch Oak's nimbleness in action. Someone that big and strong should not be so light on their feet.

Oak planted his feet and punched down at Hok'ee. The skinwalker danced out of the way as Oak's massive fist struck the ground, flinging dirt and loose pebbles around. I noticed that the displaced dirt had conveniently smothered the nearest patch of flames. Even locked in a battle of life and death, Oak was still defending the forest. Hok'ee pivoted and slashed at Oak's arm, leaving deep, bloody gashes in his skin. Oak let out an ursine roar and swatted Hok'ee away with the force of a wrecking ball. Hok'ee yelped on impact and flew through the air, colliding with a tree ten feet in the air. The weakened burning tree cracked and toppled over as the skinwalker landed on his feet and charged at the sasquatch.

During their exchange, I'd managed to rise to my feet and find my polearm. I aimed it at the skinwalker and gathered power into it for all I was worth. I took a deep breath and shouted "*Kaze!*"

Wind ripped and roared from the tip of the polearm. It manifested as a horizontal tornado that kicked up leaves, loose branches, and rocks that all hurtled towards the skinwalker. The vortex robbed the air of oxygen and the nearest flames quietly burned themselves out. My magical attack struck home, I raised my polearm, angling the gale into the air and sending the skinwalker high into the trees. The winds died out and I wobbled, trying to keep my balance through the lightheadedness.

I squinted up into the trees. "Where'd he go?"

Oak closed his eyes, then opened them a moment later. "It seems the skinwalker has fled. He was outnumbered." He gestured to the writhing flames of the dying ritual. "And his spell has failed."

I frowned, looking from Oak to the dying flames of the ritual. "Would he really give up that easily?"

Oak didn't answer. Instead he turned his attention to the out of control inferno I'd caused. He huffed out an irritated breath before he took a wide stance and began oscillating his arms. The fire that surrounded us suddenly shifted, seemingly being drawn in by whatever magic Oak was performing. The flames extended and began shifting into strands of orange light, gathering around Oak's center. He closed his hands around the tangle mess of magic and then with a swift motion, he thrust his huge arms into the air. The amber energy erupted into flames once more, transforming into a geyser of flame that shot up past the trees and briefly lighting up the immediate area so brightly, I'd almost thought the sun had risen. I caught a glimpse of the scarred landscape I'd created and another icy pang of guilt settled in the pit of my stomach. Then, the fire was gone and we were plunged back into darkness.

"You do not survive hundreds of years as a supernatural predator by fighting losing battles." Oak said, continuing the previous conversation as if he hadn't just performed an incredible feat of magic like it was a practiced circus act. He didn't even comment on the forest fire I'd caused, which made me feel even guiltier.

I shrugged, still stunned by the impressive display of magic. "Uh, fair enough."

"But I do not think this is the last time you'll run into him or his kind." Oak said. "Things that live a long time, they hold grudges better than most."

"So you're saying I just made another near-immortal enemy?"

Oak nodded. "That would be a safe assumption."

I sighed. "Not to mention, I'm sure it's not the last I've seen of these bozos either." I hooked my thumb behind me.

Oak straightened his shoulders and smiled smugly. "Noticed them, did you?"

"Yeah." I scoffed out a laugh.

Oak and I stood there quietly, waiting. Crickets began chirping, another sign the skinwalker had fled the area. But nothing else moved or made a sound.

I sighed. "Guys, seriously. I know you're there."

A moment later, leaves crunched underfoot as a dozen men emerged from the woods around us.

Chapter 13

The Aegis agents approached with guns raised and their flashlights lighting up the surrounding area. A couple of them rattled off some official sounding, hit squad mumbo jumbo, but I paid them no mind. Agent Bardot lifted his visor and approached until he stood six feet away.

"I could have you arrested, you know?" Bardot said.

"For what?" I chuckled. "Oh, did you bring Mulder and Scully this time? I was hoping they could sign my shirt."

"Interfering with an investigation, harboring a fugitive, assaulting an officer." Bardot listed. "Should I go on?"

"I called up some mist. That's hardly assault." I corrected him. "And you guys saw what just went down, right? You were too busy hunting my big friend here, you almost let a skinwalker pull off a creepy death ritual. But we took care of it, you're welcome."

Bardot frowned. "You've got a smart mouth kid, you know that?"

"It goes well with my sparkling personality." I gave him an innocent look, batting my eyelashes for effect. Then I placed my hands on my hips. "Don't you have to get back to checking the parking meters back at the park's home office or something?

"We could still take that big, ugly bastard in." Bardot thrust his chin up at Oak, completely ignoring my jab.

"For what?" I snapped.

"He's a supernatural creature found at the scene of multiple murders used for some sort of ritual." Bardot said smartly. "We have grounds to take him in. You as well, if we wanted to."

I scowled at him and closed the distance between us. Several guns clicked into position, all aimed at me as I did so. I eyed them back and forth. "Really guys? I just threw a skinwalker into orbit and you're pointing guns at me?"

I stood confidently, like I could kick all their asses with one arm tied behind my back. Truthfully, that many guns pointed at me nearly made me shit myself, but I couldn't let them know that. I locked eyes with Bardot, daring him to start something.

Bardot stared back at me for a second longer, then looked away. "Okay, let's wrap it up boys. The target got away. We'll get 'em next time."

The heavily armed agents lowered their weapons and started to clear out. Crisis averted. The fight with the skinwalker had really worn me out. I wasn't too sure I could take them all on in a straight up fight. At least not without being riddled by bullets in the process. Even with He Who Walks Among the Oaks and Listens to their Whispers on my side.

Bardot looked back to me. "Be seeing you, Mr. Leight." He flipped his visor back down and followed after his men into the woods.

Oak chuckled. "Expertly done. You are coming into the ways of a wizard quite well, young one."

"The tornado thing? Yeah I've had that one down for a couple years." I waved dismissively.

Oak shook his head. "Not what I mean."

I looked at him, confused.

"A wizard's greatest weapon is deception and strategy." Oak said. "Power is one thing, but it is the power you are perceived to have that will really make your enemies uneasy. Bardot believed you were a threat capable of taking on his entire squad, when you were clearly spent after your battle with the skinwalker."

I nodded, filing that information somewhere safe in my head. Then I looked around at the ruined ritual area. I frowned. "Hey uh, do you think you could help me get back to my car?" I spun a finger around, gesturing at our surroundings. "All these trees kinda look the same."

Oak smiled, amused. "Fear not, wizard. I know the way." He began walking off in a direction I was pretty sure wasn't the right way. But hey, for all I knew, that was just a sign I needed his help that much more.

After about an hour's walk in the woods, we arrived in the parking lot where I'd parked Mr. Williams' Beetle. I took a few steps out of the forest before turning to face Oak. I frowned. He was standing at the edge of the tree line, purposely not leaving the boundaries of the forest.

"This is where I leave you, Mr. Leight." Oak said.

"Uh, just Tobias is fine." I said. "Thank you, He Who Walks Among the Oaks and Listens to their Whispers. Without you, I'd probably have been a skinwalker's dinner."

"I should be the one thanking you, Tobias." Oak said. "I would not have been able to sabotage the skinwalker's plans on my own. Especially not with those mortal agents trying to hunt me down."

"Yeah seriously, they were quite the piece of work." I chuckled. "Bunch of bozos, wandering aimlessly around the woods waving their guns around."

"Do not underestimate them. The Aegis Institute has become more active and more competent over the years. Left unchecked, they could become a serious threat to all of supernatural kind." Oak said seriously.

I pondered that for a moment. Sure, they seem heavily armed. But they had barely been able to track Oak or the skinwalker down. And even then, they'd probably only happened upon either of them because of my clumsy human presence. Oak had shown that he could move through the woods without a sound. It wouldn't surprise me if the skinwalker had similar abilities.

"I'll keep it in mind." I pointed over my shoulder to the Beetle. "I should get back but, keep in touch?"

Oak nodded. "Yes, I think we will see each other again, Tobias. Times are changing, and the few good souls left in the world will need every ally they can muster."

"Uh, should I give you my phone number or something? Do you even have a phone?" I asked clumsily.

Oak let out a big, belly laugh. His whole body shuddered with the energy of it. "Worry not wizard, when you are in need of me, or I of you, we will find each other."

Without another word, the Bigfoot lumbered back into the woods. His form seemed to fade into the brush like a mirage. Before I knew it, he was gone completely. Someday, I would need him to teach me that trick. But for now, it was time to make the long drive home. I stretched my arms into the air, trying to rid my body of the leftover tension and exhaustion. The bruises I got from this little excursion would be ones to remember for sure.

I let out a huff of breath and made my way to the Volkswagen Beetle that I'd parked there earlier in the night and prepared for the night of torture by radio I'd have to endure.

Journey to the Center of the Underworld

Bishop Leight is the guardian wizard of Seattle, but his job takes him to some strange places. When High Elder Braun calls asking for a favor, Bishop answers the call to action. This story takes place two years before the events of *Fallen Son*.

Chapter 14

Allow me to introduce myself. I am Bishop Rodrick Sebastian Leight, a seasoned wizard of the Mystic Order, stationed in the rainy city of Seattle. Over the course of two centuries, I have dedicated my life to mastering the arcane arts. Each day, I rise before the sun, relishing in the tranquility of the early morning. It is a time when the mortal world slumbers, and the creatures of the night retreat to their shadows. This, my friends, is my favorite part of the day.

I made my way downstairs soundlessly, where the coffee pot was just about finished brewing one of man's greatest creations. The machine's burble died down as it finished dispensing the dark roast into the pot. I pulled a mug from the cabinet and filled it with the awaiting elixir. I took my full mug and set it on the small table next to my recliner, making sure to use a coaster, of course. Then I made my way to the front door, where the morning paper was already waiting for me. I paid extra to make sure that it was delivered nice and early so I could read it while the world was still quiet. This routine, a testament to my discipline and dedication, has been my anchor for years.

I took a seat in my recliner, deploying the leg rest as I unfurled the morning paper. With the newspaper propped between one hand and my lap, I sipped carefully at the steaming hot mug. This has been my routine for years and I never grew tired of it. I preferred the old-school method of getting my daily news, as opposed to the morning news on television. News channels were far too focused on political nonsense and fluff pieces. While I enjoyed the occasional feel-good story of firefighters saving a cat from a tree or the latest political scandal, I much rather read the paper so I could pick and choose what I learned about the goings-on in the world. This way, I could stay informed without being overwhelmed by the noise of the world.

Moreover, it was part of my duty. I'd been appointed as a protector of sorts of Seattle and the greater Washington area. Years of trials and tribulations against the supernatural had proven my abilities sufficient to keep a watchful eye over my territory. When one of the many supernatural factions got out of line, or a rogue troll caused trouble, it was my solemn duty to deal with the issue. It was crucial that matters of the supernatural were kept under wraps and out of the public eye.

Humanity, as a whole, had grown ignorant of the supernatural world around them—happily so, even. Mankind was terrified of things they did not understand, and as we advanced as a species, we became more reliant on technology and mundane, scientific expectations of how the world worked. This meant that mankind's understanding and reverence for the supernatural became nothing more than superstition and fairy tales to tell children before bed.

Which left the mighty few to remain vigilant against anything that went bump in the night. So, I read the paper. You'd be surprised what supernatural activity was reported in the paper, even if the journalists didn't know exactly what they were reporting. Reports of kidnappings and animal attacks were occasionally the work of a troll, black dog, or other supernatural predator, rather than some other ne'er-do-well. On even rarer occasions, Mystic Order agents within law enforcement would pass a case on to me as well. It was my job to discern the supernatural from the mundane and deal with them accordingly. It was rare that any of these cases actually panned out; nevertheless, it was an obligation of mine to keep an eye on such things.

It was a half hour before sunrise when my cell phone rang. It was an old Nokia flip phone, as I had little need for the various odds and ends of the newer smartphones that had become so prevalent. My nephew liked to call the device a "vintage model."

I recognized the number immediately and flipped open the phone, holding it to my ear. "Good morning, High Elder Braun."

Braun's German accent came through clearly. "Oh dear, is it morning? Forgive me, Bishop. Too much time in Light Haven can play tricks on one's perception of time. Did I wake you?"

I cracked a smile. Roland Braun was not someone you'd expect to be the man in charge of the Mystic Order, the government body for all wizards. He was an old man, much older than me. But he had the spirit of someone a fraction of his age.

"No sir, I was already up." I eased his worries.

"Good to hear," Braun said. "Anyways, I'm calling because I have a matter to discuss."

When he said matter, he usually meant a problem of some kind that he needed solving.

"I see, and you think I can help you with this problem?"

"Yes, I think your past experiences make you the right man for the job," Braun said. "Better to not discuss the details over the phone. How soon can you be at Light Haven?"

I looked at the clock on the wall and considered how long it would take me to get to Seattle's gateway to Light Haven. "Give me an hour or so, and I'll be there."

I could practically see Braun nodding as he spoke. "Good, good. I'll see you then."

The line clicked as Braun hung up. I clicked the phone shut and folded my newspaper. Usually, I was the one seeking out the work. But it appeared that this time around, the work had sought me out. I took a few minutes to finish my coffee and mull over the prospect of an upcoming mission. It was not often that Braun called me personally to handle any sort of matter. I was on the payroll, sure, but the Mystic Order had special agents, known as Sentinels, who usually handled such issues.

If Braun was calling me for assistance, it meant he wanted something handled discreetly. Which meant that someone had messed up. I grinned, letting out a chuckle. As I rose to get ready, I contemplated just what kind of mess the High Elder had found himself in.

I got myself ready, making sure to move quietly so as not to wake my nephew from his slumber. My nephew, Tobias, knew nothing of the supernatural or his heritage, not yet at least. It was always a bit tricky to sneak away on one of my missions when he was awake, so I was thankful that I wouldn't have to worry about it this time.

My ensemble consisted of a tan Henley shirt, dark jeans, steel-toed hiking boots, and a thick denim jacket with plenty of pockets. I went out to my garage, which served as my study, where I kept all of my various wizarding implements. My staff leaned against the wall in the far corner. With a flick of my wrist and a whispered word, the staff flew across the room and into my outstretched hand.

I debated bringing along some of the various other minor magic artifacts kept in the garage. After a moment of deliberation, I grabbed a small white jewel attached to a leather cord and deposited it into one of my jacket's many pockets. Sitting on the table in the center of the room was a coiled length of white rope. I looped it through my belt and made sure it was secure but easily accessible.

Satisfied, I decided it was time to get moving. I exited the apartment, ensuring the door was locked, and the protective wards were fully functional. As I began my walk to Light Haven's local entrance, I sent my nephew a text message explaining my absence. I maintained a flexible day job to cover for my various disappearances. I wrote for a small science fiction and fantasy magazine, contributing short stories here and there. Whenever I had to leave for Mystic Order business, I explained that I was at a writer's conference or a meeting at the magazine's office. It hadn't failed me yet.

My apartment complex was technically a townhouse complex, but I'd yet to meet anyone who was willing to correct me. Unfortunately, Seattle proper was not built to accommodate any non-vertical apartment dwellings, which meant it was quite a walk to Pike Place, where the hidden entrance to Light Haven was located. I didn't bother with a car, because any and every car I'd owned over the years had met a terrible fate. My cars had been crushed, ripped apart, and even blown up by various monsters and adversaries I'd gone up against over the years. And as time went on, it became more and more expensive to replace them.

So I walked. It was a healthy habit to keep anyway. It took me about an hour or so to reach Pike Place. The sun shone on the horizon and bathed the world in early morning light. The hustle and bustle of the city was just now starting to pick up. Locals were running off to their jobs, and tourists hurried to stand in line at the first-ever location of a major coffee chain.

My destination was the historic Gum Wall. The Gum Wall itself had some disgusting yet charming history, and it was one of many must-see tourist spots in the city. But I frequented it for an entirely different reason. I opened my wizard senses. As I did, several pieces of dried chewing gum seemed to glow with a white light. I pressed each piece like a button. Once I'd input the proper sequence, a glowing doorway opened up before me. It was early enough that no tourists were here to witness this, not that they could anyhow. The Gum Wall had special veils worked into it that hid the secret entrance into Light Haven. I walked through the doorway, and after a moment of being blinded by a bright light, I found myself in the Mystic Order's headquarters; Light Haven.

Wizards from all over the world hurried around me, coming in and out of doors that led to other secret doorways all across the continent. There was no consistency between the wizards' appearances. Some wore traditional robes and hoods. Others wore more casual, modern clothing, like myself. I knew of one wizard from Texas who dressed like a cowboy straight off the set of Walker, Texas Ranger.

I walked through the crowd towards the hallway that would lead deeper into Light Haven, my staff echoing on the tile floor as I moved. The many, many, many halls of Light Haven were a labyrinth of seemingly infinite size and could be very confusing to someone who wasn't used to their quirks. The halls seemed to change and rearrange themselves constantly, and it took some time to get used to their habits. But I'd been doing this for a while now, and my master, Wizard Henry Killian, had made sure that I knew my way around Light Haven before he ever taught me serious magic.

I navigated Light Haven's halls with ease as I headed toward Braun's office. The deeper you went into the halls, the fewer wizards, dwarves, and elves you'd come across. It wasn't until you were close to your destination that more and more people would appear again.

Braun was a man of the people, and thus, he kept his office amongst some of the lowest-ranked members of Light Haven's staff. I emerged in a large room filled with cubicles. Along the outer walls, there were glass-enclosed offices where some of the higher-ups worked as well. This was Light Haven's financial office, where various members worked on all things related to the Mystic Order's finances. The Mystic Order had many small businesses, big businesses, and stock investments that kept it funded. You'd be surprised to find out what companies and organizations were actually fronts for the Mystic Order.

The cubicles were primarily occupied by wizards with a small talent for magic. These were wizards who knew a few small tricks but weren't strong enough to be among the ranks of Protectors, like me, and especially not Sentinels. This was where Roland Braun chose to keep his office. Like I said, he was a big fan of the little guy. His office was one of the glass-enclosed ones in the far corner of the room. The walls were dominated by large windows that showed various sceneries of The World Yonder. It changed every day or two. Today, the windows displayed a vibrant grassland of too-green grass and floating wisps of light that moved across the landscape lazily.

I approached Braun's office and saw that he was focused on some documents strewn across his desk. Braun was a man of dark skin and rough, time-worn features. He wore his hair in long, graying dreadlocks. The top two buttons of his maroon dress shirt were unbuttoned and he'd taken off his tie at some point. The man looked stressed.

I knocked on the open glass door. "Hello, High Elder."

Braun looked up from his papers and smiled with bright white teeth. "Bishop, thank you for coming!" His words were tinged with a faint German accent.

"I came as soon as I could."

"Good, good. As I said on the phone, I have a concerning matter I was hoping you could help me with."

"What's the problem?" I asked him.

Braun brandished a playful smile at my choice of words. Whenever it came to matters he needed me to handle, I always changed the word to problem. It was one of the small ways I enjoyed teasing the High Elder. It wasn't something many could get away with, so I made sure to take advantage of it.

"Well, I'll give it to you straight," Braun said, his voice becoming grave. "I need you to go to the Underworld."

Chapter 15

"The Underworld? You're going to have to be a little more specific." I said.

In truth, many underworlds and, by extension, afterlives were said to exist. No one was quite sure how it all worked, given that many people believed in many different afterlives. Many other people didn't believe in any afterlife at all. And even then, many afterlives went by different names and were represented differently depending on the name. Hel, the Duat, Purgatory, Xibalba, Rarohenga, just to name a few. They all represented the underworld in different cultures, all with wildly different beliefs in their purpose.

"You may be familiar with this one. I'm, of course, talking about Hades." Braun clarified.

Ah, so that's why Braun had requested me specifically to help him. As a wizard, I'd dealt with my fair share of supernatural and mythological trials. But for some reason, the Greeks kept popping up time and time again. It was only a few years ago that I'd found myself facing off against the Gorgons Three. That had been an exciting weekend.

"So did you drop something in the River Styx?" I asked him.

He ignored the jab. "No, nothing quite so tame. You know of the Aegis Institute, correct?"

I grunted.

The Aegis Institute was a secret government organization that specializes in all things supernatural. They killed monsters, acquired artifacts, and conducted all sorts of experiments to weaponize the supernatural in order to serve humanity—or so it liked to say. In reality, it was primarily for getting the one-up on the United States' enemies.

"My sources say that a team of Aegis agents was spotted opening a gateway. Further investigation revealed that it was a gateway into the Underworld." Braun explained. "Whatever they're planning to do there can't be good. And the last thing we need is for them to accidentally stir one the God who slumbers there."

"So you want me to...what? Scare them off?" I asked.

"Yes, but there's one more thing." Braun added.

I sighed. Of course, there was. There was always one more thing.

"I was hoping while you were there, you could bring back a Pomegranate." Braun requested.

I narrowed my eyes. "You want a Pomegranate from the Underworld? What for?"

"We were hoping to study its magical properties and how they could be used in medicine." He said.

"Mhmm," I grumbled.

The Pomegranates of the Greek Underworld were said to have many magical properties, but the Mystic Order knew nothing outside of myths and legends. In our line of work, myths and legends often point to fact. It was just never clear what to believe and what to dismiss. However, the most prevalent piece of information the Mystic Order was confident in was the Pomegranate's power to bind a god.

I mulled that thought over for a moment. Could it be possible that the Mystic Order could be trying to bind a god to prevent it from awakening? A darker part of me considered the fact that the Mystic Order might actually try to bind a god to their will. But I thought better of it. It didn't fit. The Mystic Order did whatever they could to keep the sleeping gods of the old world quiet and contained. The modern world would not fare well if gods started waking up to reclaim the Earth.

"So, Bishop, will you help me?" Braun asked.

I nodded. "Yes, I think I can help."

Like all mythological realms, the Greek Underworld was located somewhere in The World Yonder. The World Yonder was an alternate dimension theorized to be the size of or much larger than our own universe. It was impossible to map, and it always shifted and changed. But it had a tendency to connect with our world at related points. And given the right circumstances and ingredients, you could open a portal to exactly where you needed to go.

My venture into the underworld began at Black Diamond Cemetery, about an hour away from Seattle. It was inconvenient as hell to go an hour out of the way, but Black Diamond was said to be home to many restless spirits. The spirits in question being miners from way back when. Along with my other materials for the gateway spell, I was hoping the subterranean parallels would give me an edge in the spell.

I exited the taxi and tipped the driver generously, grunting as I hauled my duffel bag out of the car. The taxi drove off as I turned to face the cemetery. The moon shone brightly in the clear night sky. The cemetery was a modest place, corralled only by a waist-height chain link fence. Under the moonlight, I could just make out several tombstones of various shapes and sizes in the distance. I hopped over the fence and headed for the approximate center of the cemetery. It wasn't huge, as cemeteries go, less than half the size of a football field.

As I walked, I caught flickers of movement out of the corner of my eye. I didn't expect any visitors, but that didn't mean I'd drop my guard. If anything, my visitors wouldn't be of the living, breathing variety. Black Diamond Cemetery was a hot spot for paranormal activity. There were countless sightings of phantoms and shadow figures over the years. But nothing of consequence, as far as the Mystic Order was concerned. The spirits here were restless, but they hadn't demonstrated themselves to be malicious. So long as I didn't do anything to upset them, I suspected they'd let me work unimpeded.

After a ten-minute walk, I stopped to scan my surroundings. The location was relatively clear of tombstones or memorials, so I was most likely free of the restless spirits' wrath. With that settled, I got to work. I used a can of spray paint to draw a circle on the grass. With a simple touch and a whispered word, I empowered the circle. It snapped to life and an inaudible buzz of energy began to tickle my arcane senses.

Then I spread out the implements I'd brought along. First, I poured out several drachma coins from a leather pouch. Next, a pendant that resembled an old vase with dolphin-shaped handles, and finally, I unsheathed a restored Greek kopis. The blade was a genuine original that I'd been restoring over the years. It took a lot of careful, steady magic work and I'd planned to enchant it for combat use, but I'd yet to get around to it.

With the artifacts spread around the circle, I began to chant. I muttered ancient Greek syllables as I focused on gathering more and more energy into the circle. I moved my arms back and forth in a circular motion, imagining a whirlpool in my mind's eye. It took several minutes, and after only a couple, my aging muscles began to protest. But the well of power was forming just as I'd hoped, like a broth swirling in a cooking pot. When the spell reached its boiling point, I opened my eyes and shouted a word.

"*Thýra!*" My voice echoed.

The magic surged and suddenly coalesced into visible light. The light formed into a disc of energy, the light at its center slowly receding to reveal a landscape on the other side. Through the gateway, I saw a bleak world made up of cliffs and barren gray earth. There was a heavy mist hanging over the scenery and despite there being no sun to light the landscape, there was an eerie silver glow that gave the world some semblance of light.

I'd done it. I had opened a gate to the Underworld.

I stepped through the gateway and the temperature instantly dropped by twenty degrees. I shivered and puffed out a breath, trying to push the cold sensation to the back of my mind. Despite what popular media would tell you, the Greek Underworld was not a fiery hellscape scarred with lava flows and demonic monsters flying around. It was dark and devoid of color. Most of the landscape was barren and there wasn't a soul, living or dead, in sight.

There was a faint thudding sound at the edge of my hearing. At first, I was confused as to what it was. I scanned my surroundings hoping to find the sound's source. It was only after a couple of minutes did I realize that the sound wasn't coming from my surroundings. The Underworld was dead silent, no pun intended. What I was hearing was the sound of my own blood pumping. That realization was only slightly disconcerting.

I tried to ignore the sensation, instead focusing on what I was going to do next. I'd made it into the underworld, sure. But I had no idea where to go next. The landscape had no distinguishing landmarks. I rubbed my chin, trying to think of my next course of action.

Somebody shuffled past me, brushing against my shoulder as they went.

"Oh, sorry," I muttered absentmindedly.

After a couple of seconds, the absurdity of what just happened hit me like a train. I did a double-take, looking up to the figure shuffling along down the hill I stood on. The figure was a man, wearing an old ruffled business suit. His hair was dark and unkempt, but his most notable feature was the glowing white aura that hung around him like a cloud.

The man was a ghost, a spirit passed on. For one reason or another, this is the afterlife he'd ended up in. I racked my brain, trying to recall my knowledge of Greek mythology. The ghost was walking in a straight line towards a ravine. Upon further observation, I noted several other glowing figures in the distance. More ghosts, most likely. They were all heading somewhere, clearly. Since I didn't have a better course of action, I decided it wouldn't hurt to follow them. I memorized the gateway's location and closed it with a small effort. I didn't want to risk anyone or anything else coming in or out of the gate.

Then, I began following the growing crowd of ghosts into the ravine. They didn't seem to notice me, or if they did, they didn't care one way or another about my presence. I did my best to keep my distance from the spirits while following them. Even so, they still occasionally bumped into me.

Keeping proper track of time anywhere in The World Yonder was a challenge. The flow of time was constantly changing and was never in sync with the material world. For all I knew, I could've been walking for two minutes or two hours. It worried me that I might potentially be away from my nephew for extended periods of time. But he was used to my extended absences, and should anything happen to me; there were contingencies in place to make sure he was cared for in the long run.

Finally, I saw what the spirits had been heading for. After walking through the ravine for an indeterminate amount of time, it opened up onto a sandy shore. The water was gray and lifeless, like everything else, and it flowed lazily downhill into the mist. Someone was waiting for the wandering spirits. A large canoe-style boat of pitch-black wood was beached at the edge of the river, and the figure was at its helm. The figure was shrouded entirely by a worn, gray cloak. I couldn't see his face, only one of his hands, which held a long oar that matched the boat's pure-black color.

It took me a moment, but I realized who this figure probably was. Charon, the ferryman of the dead. If I was right, that made the river before me the River Styx. I shouldered past the milling spirits and took a closer look at the river itself. The water flowed slowly, and upon closer inspection, I noticed that there were faces in the water. They came in and out of focus, their expressions locked in terror and despair. As soon as a face appeared it would be gone again. Hundreds, maybe thousands, of faces were trapped within the Styx's waters. These too, were forlorn spirits. Perhaps they couldn't afford to pay the ferryman.

I felt a prickling sensation on my neck. Someone was watching me. I turned to where Charon stood on his boat. Sure enough, his shadowed hood was facing my direction. He didn't move, didn't even twitch. The ferryman stood stone still, simply observing me.

Then he spoke.

"You do not belong here, wizard," Charon said.

His voice was strange. As if it were composed of thousands of whispering voices all saying the same thing. Some of the whispers were behind or ahead by a syllable or two, so it was a bit of a challenge to understand exactly what the ferryman was saying.

I cleared my throat, standing and approaching the ferryman.

"My apologies for the intrusion, honored Charon. My name is Bishop Leight, I'm a wizard of the Mystic Order," I said, lacing my words with reverence. "But I've come to your master's honored land because there are more trespassers than just myself. I've been tasked with sending them on their way, so as not to upset the balance of this realm."

I made sure not to mention my secondary mission, that of acquiring one of the Underworld's Pomegranates. I didn't think Charon would take too kindly to me if I let that vital piece of information slip.

Charon seemed to mull this over for a moment. "Yes, other men have trespassed upon the realm of Hades. Mortal soldiers, they seek something in these lands, yes?"

"We believe so," I nodded.

"They will not fare well here. There are many dangers that call this land home," Charon said.

"Even so, I cannot allow them to remain here and enact whatever plans they have," I said. "All I request is that you grant me safe passage for my time here."

Charon cocked his head to one side, as if deep in thought. Then he turned his attention back to me. "I cannot guarantee you safe passage, wizard. The realm of Hades is its own being and will deal with you however it sees fit. However, if you pay the toll, I can guarantee you passage across the River Styx so you may continue your journey. In return for thwarting these trespassers, I will ferry you back across once your mission is complete."

I had a feeling that was going to be Charon's best offer.

"Very well, honored Charon," I tilted my head forward respectfully. Then I reached into my duffel bag and pulled out several of the remaining drachma I'd put aside. I'd had a feeling I'd be meeting Charon on my journey, so I wanted to be prepared.

Charon held out his hand, and I deposited the drachma. He seemed to examine them before tucking them away in his cloak. Then, he motioned for me to climb aboard his ferry. Several other spirits gave the ferryman their payment. How so many people had drachma to pay with in the afterlife, I didn't know. Perhaps he accepted other forms of payment. Maybe the Underworld had gotten with the times, and Charon accepted PayPal.

With his ferry loaded with ghosts and one wizard, the ferryman pushed off the shore with his oar and began guiding the boat through the waters of the River Styx.

179

Chapter 16

Riding a ferry full of ghosts across the River Styx did not make for a calming experience. The river was flowing fast and behaved unpredictably. It acted more like a restless ocean rather than a river, and it was seemingly just as vast. I estimated we'd been traveling for nearly an hour, but I still couldn't see the other side. I wasn't the only one feeling uneasy, the spirits bustled and shuffled about, bumping into each other and me. Though they couldn't touch me, the sensation of their intangible bodies passing through mine sent chills down my spine. I wasn't one to let nerves get to me, but my experience on Charon's ferry was starting to push it.

I crossed my arms and closed my eyes, trying to focus on my own thoughts. Soon, I'd be across the River Styx and one step closer to tracking down the agents from the Aegis Institute. I had to wonder what they were doing here or how they even got here. The Aegis Institute had been around in one form or another since the late 1700s, but there'd never been much to worry about. But now it seemed they were starting to grow bold, no longer content with defending humanity against supernatural incursions. Now, they were making moves into their enemy's territory. They thought they knew best, but they were meddling with things they couldn't possibly understand. One wrong move, and they could have an angry god on our heels.

The front of the boat jerked as it hit something, nearly knocking me off balance. I shifted my feet to keep myself upright and looked to see what we'd hit. To my relief, we'd arrived at the opposite shore. The ghostly passengers were already disembarking. I waited for the boat to clear out before I moved. Charon stood stoically at the boat's helm as I passed him by. As I disembarked, I nodded respectfully towards the ferryman.

Charon gave no response, instead seemingly watching the spirits wander to their next destination. I wondered if he was trying to tell me something. I turned to watch the crowd of wandering ghosts and decided my best course of action was to follow them. What could possibly go wrong?

Ghosts were not great conversationalists. I'd been having a one-sided conversation with the one specter that had been keeping pace with me. It paid me no attention, which was fine enough. I was only maintaining the conversation for my own sake. The eerie silence and isolation of the Underworld could have easily driven me insane.

My voice trailed off when I experienced an unfamiliar sensation in the underworld. I *heard* something—and not just anything. I ceased my yammering and listened closely. Unless I had gone insane, I was pretty sure I was hearing the distant sound of gunfire—automatic weapons, to be specific. I assumed there wouldn't be many other groups toting automatic weapons in the underworld. That was most definitely the sound of Aegis agents.

I broke off from the parade of spirits, headed in the direction where the gunfire was coming from. As I got closer, I could hear people shouting back and forth, though I couldn't tell what they were saying. That's when I heard the enraged leonine roar of some large, angry creature. That couldn't possibly be good.

I held my arm out as I ran and performed an intricate twisting motion with my wrist and fingers. One moment, my hand was empty. And in the next, a six-foot-long staff made of dark oak appeared in my grip. My staff was gnarled and misshapen, but I always thought that just gave it more character. Runes from several different languages and cultures were carved into the wood. As I tightened my grip on the staff, the runes began to glow with an eerie purple light. I focused on my breathing as I ran, both to conserve my stamina and the steady breathing helped me gather my magic. I had a feeling I'd need to let loose in just a few seconds.

As I crested the last hill, I saw what all the commotion was about. Several men were dressed in tactical gear, all of them brandishing automatic weapons. But what they were surrounding really caught my interest. The behemoth was somewhere around twelve feet tall, from foot to shoulder. It had the general build of a bulldog but was obviously much bigger. It was completely hairless, with charcoal-black skin covering its entire body. Where its forepaws should've been, it had fists instead, and it bounded around much like a gorilla. Its gigantic maw was full of misshapen, mismatched, razor-sharp teeth, and a streak of flame ran from the top of its head and down its spine.

"Hellhound," I whispered.

I observed the conflict further. The hellhound was giving them hell, no pun intended. It batted away its attackers with ease. I noted several bodies which lay crumpled on the ground...in several pieces. What the hell had gotten into these Aegis agents? Why were they attacking a full-grown hellhound on its home turf?

I saw a flash of steel, and several of the remaining agents brandished chains, preparing to throw them. Meanwhile, several other agents were still pestering the hellhound with their weapons. The guns wouldn't have much luck harming the hellhound, but maybe that wasn't the point. Several shouts rang out, followed by the glint of steel flying through the air. Before long, the Aegis agents had managed to pin the creature and were working on binding its limbs. The beast wasn't giving up without a fight. It struggled for all it was worth, pulling on the chains and snapping at them with its teeth.

The hellhound may have been much bigger and stronger than the puny agents, but it was outnumbered and outmaneuvered. I supposed it was time to even the odds.

I gripped my staff in both hands and spun it clockwise. As I did so, I shouted: "*Igni orbita!*"

Twelve balls of purple flame appeared along the arc of my staff's movement. With another flourish of my staff, I sent the fireballs hurtling down towards the Aegis agents. The fireballs exploded against my targets and flung them away. I heard cries of pain and surprise from the agents. The fireballs I'd conjured weren't very deadly. I'd only packed enough energy into them to fling the agents away while disorienting and singing them.

The hellhound tugged itself free of the chains and let out a bellowing roar as the Aegis agents scrambled to recover. The beast's eyes landed on me. It seemed to look me over, and I could see understanding in its eyes as it put two and two together. The Aegis agents were on their feet again and had weapons trained on the hellhound. But I was quicker.

I swept my staff across my body, shouting, "*Magnes!*"

The dozen or so agents' firearms suddenly flew from their hands and floated in a nebulous pile above the tip of my staff. I smiled, a hint of mocking pride in my expression. The hellhound let out another roar and then began bounding away. It didn't take long before the hellhound had disappeared into the mist.

With the hellhound safely away, I swept my staff again, releasing my spell. Their weapons clattered to the ground in a heap, safely out of their hands. I flourished my staff once and then tapped it against the ground, releasing a burst of energy by my feet. It was purely for showmanship purposes. I didn't want these Aegis agents getting any bright ideas about picking a fight with me.

One of the agents said something to the others that I couldn't make out and then started climbing the hill towards me. He hadn't bothered to pick up his weapon, so I was pretty sure he wasn't coming up here in an attempt to kill me. Nevertheless, I remained on guard. The agent pressed a button on his helmet, and his high-tech visor retreated into his helmet, revealing his eyes to me. A moment later, the helmet's mouthpiece retracted as well.

The agent's appearance was...very boring. He was seemingly of average build, though it was hard to tell under all the tactical gear he wore. He was of average height, so a few inches shorter than me. His face had no blemishes to speak of. The only less-than-boring thing about him was his absolutely striking gray eyes.

"Sir, you're interfering with a—" The agent began.

"I don't want to hear it," I snapped. "Not. One. Bit."

The agent's face twisted. He looked absolutely baffled. I had a feeling he wasn't used to people talking to him that way. The agent probably expected me to flop over and do whatever he said. Had he forgotten the swift and firm ass whooping I'd just delivered unto him and his goon squad?

"You are the ones who do not belong here," I said. "The Underworld is not meant to be disturbed. Do you have ANY idea what the consequences could be for your incursion here, Agent...?"

"Bardot."

"Agent Bardot," I finished. "One wrong step and you could piss off an entity that your government has no ability to fight whatsoever."

Bardot raised an eyebrow at that. "You really think a Greek God could be troubled to deal with one squad of mortal agents?"

"I think the risk of it happening, however small, far outweighs whatever reward you're hoping to obtain." I answered. "Do yourselves a favor and leave. Come back through whatever portal you jury-rigged to get here and seal it shut."

"I don't take orders from you," Bardot said flatly.

"They're not orders," I said, turning to walk away. "Just advice from someone far more well-versed in this particular field of play."

I didn't get to see Bardot's face as I walked away, but his silence told me everything I needed to.

It wasn't hard for me to pick up the spirits' trail once more. Using my arcane senses, I could easily tell where the spirits had been and a rough idea where they were headed. I followed the trail at a brisk pace and eventually caught up to some stragglers from the wave of spirits that had ridden on the ferry with me. I sincerely hoped that Bardot and his agents heeded my advice. The Underworld was no place for living, breathing mortals. It was only a matter of time before something much nastier than a hellhound picked up their scent and made lunch out of them.

There were all sorts of things lurking down here. Many of them known through Greek mythology, but there were other things said to dwell on the edges of Hades. Things mankind had rarely encountered before and hopefully never would again. There were rumors and speculation that Hades existed on the outer edges of The World Yonder's infinite expanse and that it acted as a defensive wall against whatever dwelt outside those boundaries. I'd always dismissed such talk as ridiculous. Nothing could exist in the Void.

After an hour of walking through the seemingly endless landscape, the crowd of spirits seemed to slow and congregate. I looked up and saw why. The giant obsidian gates had not been there a moment ago. I was sure of it. Yet, here they were.

I frowned at the gates. For whatever reason, I hadn't given the Underworld's gates much thought in my plans. Passing through them would be difficult, considering you had to be a ghost to pass through under normal conditions. And I was not dying for the sake of this mission.

An idea popped into my head.

I reached into one of my many pockets and pulled out the white crystal hanging from a leather cord. It was the first of two new magical tools I'd been working on recently, and I figured there was no better time than now to test it out. I wrapped the leather cord around my hand and held it tight in a fist, with the crystal hanging over my hand. I gathered my power and channeled it into the crystal, my breathing slowing as I focused on the task.

"*Gāst*," I whispered.

At first, it seemed like nothing happened. Then my body suddenly felt lighter than air. I looked down at myself and noticed a faint white aura surrounding me. Additionally, my body and clothes had become slightly transparent. I grinned, the artifact worked as intended and made my body and anything I touched completely intangible. Just to be sure, I knelt down and moved to press my hand against the ground. Sure enough, my hand went right through the ground. Now that was a strange sensation. I'd stuck my hand and wrist through the ground, the affected areas of my body tingled strangely, as if my hand had fallen asleep.

I pulled my hand out of the ground and rose. Now, it was time to put the artifact through a proper test. Would it allow me to pass through the obsidian gates? There was only one way to find out. I took one step forward, and then another. Soon, I was only inches from the gates. I took a deep breath and then attempted to step through the closed gates.

Just before my intangible form would've passed through the gate, pure agony exploded throughout my body. I let out a pained cry as my body was ravaged by the gates' defensive magic. My body was locked in a rigid arc, as if electricity coursing through my veins. After an endless moment of pain and agony, the gates' magic flung me ten feet away. I crashed to the ground hard, tumbling head over heels. My tumble ended with me sprawled across the ground, face down.

Everything hurt. I cursed at myself. I should've known bypassing the obsidian gates wouldn't be so easy. They were an ancient power of the mystical world, a mortal-made artifact like my crystal had no chance of subverting their power. I gritted my teeth and rose to a kneeling position, examining myself for injuries. The obsidian gates' counter magic had canceled out my intangibility and I was solid once more. I examined the crystal that I still held by its cord. The crystal seemed undamaged. I counted myself lucky for it. I turned my attention to the gates. They towered over me with a taunting aura.

With a grunt of effort, I heaved myself to my feet and approached the gates once more. I glared at them, while I ran through ideas for possible ways to pass through the barrier. Nothing seemed feasible. I might've hit a dead end. There was nothing left to do but turn back and head home.

"Giving up so easily?" A chipper voice said.

I resisted the urge to jump out of my skin, whirling in the voice's direction directly behind me and summoning my staff in one fluid motion. I aimed the tip of the staff at the speaker, narrowing my eyes. Who the hell had so casually approached me in one of the most dangerous realms in The World Yonder?

It was a young man, leaning against one of the many giant black stones that littered the landscape. He looked to be somewhere in his mid-twenties. His hair and eyes were dark brown, but both had flecks of gold that seemed to glow in the dull darkness of the Underworld. He had perfect olive skin, free of blemishes and excess oils. He had a runner's build, well-muscled but not overly bulky. I'd seen his exact build in many long-distance and track runners over the years. The youth wore a performance tank top and lined performance shorts. The outer layer of his shorts only went to mid-thigh, revealing the compression lining underneath, which were decorated with Greek-style patterns. His running shoes were perfect white and as he pulled his leg up to stretch it out, I noticed golden wing patterns decorating the footwear.

Could it be?

The youth waved a hand and donned a friendly smile. "I'm Hermes, nice to meet'cha."

Chapter 17

I kept my staff aimed at the stranger who claimed to be a Greek God. Hermes was the god of many things, including messengers, travelers, and thieves. But he was also a trickster god; they were a key figure in mythologies all over the world, and they often acted as a check to their pantheon's power. But this man couldn't be Hermes. The gods of the old world were all in a deep sleep ever since their worshippers thinned out and eventually faded.

"Who are you?" I said, my tone short and serious.

The youth rolled his eyes amusedly. "I told you, bro. I'm Hermes. Surely, you've heard of me. Messenger god, I'm big on poetry and sports, too. I'm a bit of a jack of all trades when it comes to forms of expression. They made statues of me, y'know?"

My glare didn't waver and neither did my staff. "The old gods have been slumbering for centuries. You're no Hermes."

Again, he rolled his eyes. Then he disappeared in a streak of gold light. I whirled, preparing to unleash a deadly spell. But when I turned to meet him, he was jogging in place. His perfect smile beamed with pride and amusement.

"Does that prove it for ya?" He asked. He stopped jogging in place. "Or what about this?" He twisted his wrist, much like I did when summoning my staff from thin air. But instead of a wizard's staff, a three foot-long rod appeared in his hand. Small twin snakes twisted and spun around its length. At the top of the rod was a pair of small white wings.

It was the caduceus of Hermes. There was a sudden pressure in the air that pulsed from the god's symbol of power. I could feel a headache coming on due to the change in the air pressure. I didn't need to risk a glance at the caduceus through the magical spectrum, because who knows what that would do to my mind. The caduceus was the genuine article. Which meant...

The youth standing before me was most definitely the messenger of the gods, Hermes.

I took a step back and settled my staff, holding it by my side. "Forgive me, honored Hermes, for any disrespect I may have dealt to you." I bowed slightly in a respectful manner.

Hermes chuckled, spinning his caduceus once and resting it on his shoulder. "Don't sweat it, man. I'm not all stuck up like the rest of my family, especially ever since they all took a snooze."

"If I may ask, why are you not in a deep slumber like the rest of your brethren?" I asked him.

"Oh that's easy," He said. "For one, I was never very good at following the status quo of the other gods. Way less fun. We tricksters still have a purpose in the world, ya see? But also, sports, poetry, and commerce are still a pretty big deal all over the world. So my power didn't fade nearly as much."

I supposed that all made sense. Tricksters were a tricky facet of the supernatural world. They tended not to follow the rules of their brethren as we understood them. But they were troublemakers, as their name implied, to god and mortal alike. So the question remained, what was he doing here? And what did he want with me?

"What brings you here to the underworld?" I asked him, trying to keep my voice level and calm. In truth, the god's presence made me very uneasy. I was out of my element and while Hermes wasn't a powerhouse among the Olympians, he was still far out of my league.

"Well, among many other things, I guide lost souls on their journey through the underworld," Hermes said. "But also, I noticed that a bunch of you mortals were bumbling about my uncle's domain. So naturally, I took some time to investigate."

So he'd been watching me, as well as the Aegis agents.

"I noticed you planted your foot in those guys' asses and saved that hellhound," Hermes said. "So I figured you weren't a total asshole. Plus, I've always had a soft spot for you wizard-types. You guys are sort of like mortal tricksters."

"Does that mean you'll help me?" I asked him.

Hermes tapped his finger to his chin in thought. "I could, but it's going to cost you."

I figured as much. That was one thing that the gods and the fae had in common. Nothing ever came for free, not really. If you wanted something from one of them, they expected something in return. I did my best to avoid any debts with supernatural entities. The cost always outweighed the reward. But I had a mission to complete and I didn't see how I would surpass the obsidian gates without some divine intervention.

"What do you want from me, then?" I asked.

Hermes seemed to mull it over. "A favor for a favor sounds good to me."

That's what I'd expected. Favor for favor was a trade as old as time.

"Sometime down the line, I may need something from you." Hermes said. "And when I come a-knocking, I expect you to answer. Sounds fair?"

I nodded. "Very well."

Hermes extended an open hand.

I eyed his hand for a moment and then gripped it with my own. There was an inaudible snap as the deal was sealed. I was locked in now. If I tried to back out now, the consequences could be costly.

Hermes let go and smiled. "You had the right idea, honestly. Just not enough juice to make it work against something like the underworld's gates. Mind if I see that doohickey of yours?"

It took me a minute to realize he'd been talking about my intangibility crystal. I held it out to him. Hermes took the crystal into his hands, holding it as if it were more delicate than it actually was. He stared at it intently for a couple of moments, but nothing seemed to happen. Then he held it out to me.

"There ya go. It should get you through now. It'll get you through those gates and back before it returns to normal." Hermes explained.

I eyed the god suspiciously, taking the crystal back. I hadn't noticed any change. No surge of power, no dramatic light show. Nothing.

"You're sure it'll work?" I asked him.

Hermes held his hands out, feigning offense. "You doubt the power of the mighty and handsome Hermes?"

I cleared my throat. "My apologies. I just—"

"Expected some dramatic light show?" He said, echoing my thoughts. "Fine, give it here."

The messenger god held out his hand expectantly.

I handed it back to him. Hermes made a show of spreading his hands out over his head, a cartoon rainbow appearing between them. The crystal slid over the rainbow, going from one hand to another. There was a popping sound as the crystal rose and the rainbow morphed into a water slide. A log boat formed around the crystal, and there was a small excited cry as the log plummeted down the slide, launching into the air and landing in Hermes' open palm. The illusion disappeared, and Hermes offered the crystal to me once more.

"Feel better now?" Hermes asked, clearly amused by his antics.

I politely ignored the comment, taking the crystal back. I cleared my throat. "Thank you, Hermes,"

Hermes gave me a mock salute. "Think nothing of it." He looked at an imaginary watch on his wrist. "Well would ya look at the time. I gotta skedaddle. But I'll be seeing ya soon, wizard. And whatever you do, try not to wake up my uncle. He can get real cranky if he's woken up from his nap."

Hermes exploded into a streak of gold light that rushed past me, and then I was alone. The god was gone. Still trying to wrap my head around what had just transpired, I looked down to my intangibility artifact. Had the messenger god really given the trinket the power needed to pass through the gates?

There was only one way to find out. I wrapped the leather cord around my hand once more and concentrated on the spell. It only took a moment until I'd gathered the energy necessary to power it.

"*Gāst*," I whispered.

As before, it took a moment for the sensation to sink in. But before I knew it, I was feeling lighter than air. The nebulous white aura had formed around me once more. Nothing felt different than it had the first time I'd cast the spell. A nagging part of my brain was beginning to doubt Hermes. I took a deep breath as my eyes rose to gaze at the obsidian gates.

"Now or never, I suppose," I muttered.

Then with a hesitant first step, I approached the gate. Right when I was sure I was about to smash my nose against the gate at best, or receive another jolt of lightning at worst, it happened. I walked into the gate. Everything was dark at first, and I felt the same tingling sensation I had before. Then, next thing I knew, I was through. Whatever magic that Hermes had granted me that allowed me to pass through sputtered out almost instantly and I was tangible once more.

But I'd barely noticed, distracted by the sight before me. The world within the gates starkly contrasted the world outside its borders. The desolate, colorless landscape was replaced by a vast field of vibrant green. Wild grass that extended past my knees swayed gently in the breeze. The sky was all too blue, lit by a blazing sun. It was a truly beautiful sight. My knowledge on Greek mythology wormed its way to the forefront of my mind. Could this be Elysium, the paradise afterlife for the Greeks? It was truly beautiful. If I wasn't on a mission for the Mystic Order, I might actually stop to smell the roses, as it were. But I had something to find.

I began to wander the fields, keeping my eyes on the horizon in search of any landmarks. The breeze had a soothing quality to it. I had to fight the urge to lay down in the tall grass and take a well-deserved nap. Maybe just for a moment.

I shook my head. No, now was not the time to take a nap in a foreign afterlife. I had to focus. I had to—

A dark shape blotted out the sun as it flew over me. Something hit the ground hard, shaking it almost uncontrollably. I had to hold my arms out just to keep my balance. I looked up to see just what had ambushed me. Then I kept looking up. And up. And up.

The beast was twice the size of the hellhound I'd seen earlier. And much more ferocious. Three times as ferocious, to be exact. The monster's fine black coat shone with a healthy sheen. Its paws looked like they could crush a minivan with ease. It didn't resemble a typical hellhound, as I'd come to know them. Those were inbred abominations compared to this thing.

No, this was a purebred hellhound. The purebred hellhound. Its three pairs of glowing red eyes stared down at me with pure, unadulterated malice.

And that's when Cerberus went on the attack.

Chapter 18

I leapt away as Cerberus lunged for me. The beast brought down its paws with a mighty crash onto the spot where I'd been standing a moment before. Cerberus' three heads snapped at me as I sailed through the air, but I was just barely out of reach. I called my staff to my hand, flourishing with it once as I landed and prepared a counterattack.

I spun my staff and aimed it at Cerberus' center head. "*Igni!*"

A purple fireball exploded from the end of my staff and hurtled towards the beast. As big as the beast was, it had no chance to dodge my attack at such close range. The fireball struck true and exploded in purple fireworks. Cerberus recoiled, taking a couple of giant lumbering steps back. I didn't let up, shouting a word and flinging another ball of faerie fire at the monstrosity.

Cerberus had wised up this time around. It saw my attack coming and batted it away with one massive paw. The fireball tumbled away and exploded somewhere in the fields. I cursed and prepared another attack, but Cerberus had gone on the attack. The beast leapt for me, sailing through the air with the grace of a creature a fraction its size. I gave up on another attack and rolled out of the way, ditching my duffel bag as I did in one fluid motion. But I came up short and Cerberus was huge. The shockwave from its landing sent me flying and I landed hard on my back.

My shoulders screamed in agony as I hit the ground at an awkward angle. I was getting too old for this. I looked up just in time to see Cerberus charging toward me, shaking the ground with his every step. I rolled like my life depended on it, which it did of course.

I felt Cerberus' teeth snap against the hairs on the back of my neck, but I'd managed to roll out of the beast's reach. I found my footing, turning to face the hellish beast. Creatures as large as Cerberus may have been powerful and imposing, but they had a terrible turning radius. It took a moment for Cerberus to correct his course before he was heading for me again.

Cerberus was old and powerful and we were in his domain. One lone wizard would have a snowball's chance in hell to beat him in a fair fight. Something jostled against my waist and I looked down and saw my salvation. The rope, of course. It was no ordinary rope. It was woven from 90% unicorn hair, an extremely potent ingredient in all sorts of rituals and potions. But its most notorious property was its tactile strength.

With the right bit of magic to help, it would make the perfect leash for Cerberus. I uncoiled the rope from my belt, holding it in one hand. Cerberus was less than half a football field's length away. I aimed the tip of my staff at the ground.

"*Igni propello!*"

A combination of purple fire and kinetic force threw me fifty feet into the air in less than a second. If I timed this right, I'd land on Cerberus' back perfectly and I could bring this dog to heel. As I reached the apex of my spellbound leap, Cerberus closed in. I began to fall. This was going to be close.

I was just over his neck.

Then his back.

Then his—

I landed prone near Cerberus' backside, losing my grip on my staff as I did, and nearly fell off. I dug my fingers into his coat and hung on for all I was worth. It didn't take long for Cerberus to catch on. The beast skidded to a stop and started spinning in circles, his three heads taking turns snapping at me with those massive jaws. I decided to use his frenzy to my advantage.

The rope acted as a magical focus of sorts, much like my staff. Where my staff was meant to be tool of variety, the rope had a much more specific purpose. As I channeled bits of power into the rope's length, I felt it come alive, eager to perform its task. I just hoped it would be enough to bind the beast.

"*Praeligo*!" I shouted and tossed the rope into the air towards Cerberus' snapping jaws.

The rope writhed like an angry serpent and flashed towards Cerberus' nearest head. It dodged the hound's gnashing teeth, wrapping around its muzzle with ease before tightening and sealing the head's jaws shut. Then it went for the center head. Before long, it had bound that head's jaws as well. I might've taken a moment to stare in awe if I wasn't still holding on for dear life. The rope was working better than expected. It had completely uncoiled from my hand but was still growing in length as it went to work on the beast's final head.

The final head must've been the smarter of the three, because it had caught onto my plan. The beast's movements had become awkward and sluggish, having become disoriented when the rope had bound the first two heads, but he was now jerking and hopping around in an attempt to keep his last head free. It was an effort in vain, of course. Cerberus' movements were contradictory. While the last head was trying to stay out of reach of the rope, the other two heads were jerking his body the opposite way in an attempt to get free.

The effort was ultimately fruitless, as the rope finally got the upper hand and wrapped snugly around the final head's jaws. With Cerberus' jaws now secure, I gave the rope its next instruction with my mind and its ever growing length dove under the beast, heading for its legs. Focused on his trapped heads, Cerberus wasn't paying attention to his legs and the rope made quick work of them. Before I knew what was happening, the rope suddenly pulled taut. Cerberus tripped over himself and I was flung into the air.

I cursed myself for not planning my dismount sooner. As I tumbled through the air, I did my best to figure out the general direction of the ground. With careful timing, I held out my hand in the direction of where the ground would be in the next couple seconds.

"Ventus reductum!" I shouted, my voice growing desperate.

Without my staff in hand the spell was less focused and sloppy, but it did the trick. A blast of wind came forth and expanded, pillowing out in all directions. It slowed my impromptu flight through the air. As the spell petered out, I hit the ground. Hard enough to be uncomfortable, but soft enough so that I didn't break anything. My whole body ached and protested any further action.

"Ugh, I'm getting too old for this," I muttered to myself.

I gathered my wits and forced my protesting body to rise so I could survey my handiwork. Cerberus was a struggling heap of furry rage. The hellhound struggled against his bindings, but he'd be hard-pressed to break them. With no leverage, he had less than a snowball's chance in hell of freeing himself without aid.

I found my staff on the ground several feet away from where I'd lost it. Thankfully, Cerberus' rampage hadn't destroyed it. With it in hand once more, I approached Hades' guard dog. Three pairs of eyes locked on me as I stopped only a foot away from its center head. The poor thing was twisted awkwardly in his bindings due to his struggling. As satisfied with my handiwork as I was, I had no plans to leave him in his predicament. I needed the unicorn rope back, after all.

With the beast still and relatively calm, I had other means of temporarily incapacitating him. I raised my staff over his middle snout and whispered a word. *"Somnus,"*

I tapped the tip of my staff to his snout and watched as the subtle spell did its job. The sleep spell was meant for more human-sized foes, so I had to put some extra effort into the spell that wore me out even more. But before long, the great fluffy beast was snoring away.

I muttered the rope's recall command and it quickly slithered off the beast and coiled once more into my hand, its incredible length shrinking to its original size. I looped the rope back through my belt and surveyed my surroundings. The field truly was a peaceful place. Quiet, except for the sound of its guardian's slumber.

That's when I saw it.

My eyes widened as they fell upon the tree in the distance. I was sure it hadn't been there before, but there it was now. It was only a short walk away. Finally, my mission was nearing its end.

I approached the pomegranate tree at a leisurely pace. I kept my eyes focused on the horizon, scanning for any further threats that may try to sneak up on me. But nothing appeared. The tree itself was as mundane as they came. There was nothing remarkable about it at all. It was short as trees went, its trunk twisting up into a wide berth of leaves and fruit. Hanging from its branches were the pomegranates of legend. Presumably the very same that bound Persephone here for half of the year.

I plucked one of the pomegranates from the tree with a careful hand. The fruit too, was nothing remarkable at first glance. But I could feel a subtle power lying just under the surface. A tempting thought in the back of my mind urged me to eat it. I quickly shook it away. If one bite, one drop of juice even, passed my lips, I'd be trapped here forever. I placed the fruit in a leather pouch and deposited it into my duffel bag.

I nearly jumped out of my skin when I saw what greeted me. Ten feet away, were three elderly women sitting under a shared shawl. Elderly doesn't quite encompass the scope of just how old these three women appeared. Their skin was wrinkled far beyond what any mortal human could acquire and hung loosely over thin arms. From this distance, I couldn't make out much more detail than that. But that wasn't the most disturbing part about their sudden appearance. The three of them were working with golden thread, weaving it into something unseen amongst the dark folds of their ensemble.

Though far away, their voices echoed in my mind.

"It is almost time..." The first voice said.

"The awaited day is drawing upon us..." The second voice added.

"For the Fallen Son to rise again..." The third voice concluded.

I saw a flash of steel and felt a sudden pang of energy as they cut through the thread. Pure silence washed over us. A knot of cold dread formed deep in my core. I rushed forward, planning to question them. It was an arrogant and foolish move. No one questioned the Three Fates, the Moirai. No matter how hard I ran, how hard I pushed myself, the Moirai seemed to be just out of reach.

"Wait!" I shouted, flinging my hand out in a desperate attempt to reach them.

But before I could question the Fates further, there was the sound of cackling laughter, a gust of wind, and then the Moirai were simply gone. I stopped in my tracks, spinning to look around in an attempt to spot them. But they were gone. On that note, so was Cerberus. The slumbering beast could not have snuck away.

The fields had changed drastically with the Moirai's departure. No longer were they vibrant and peaceful. The color had drained from the world as the weather turned overcast. What the Moirai had said rattled me, and that was hard to do. Could they really know of the Fallen Son's prophecy?

It didn't matter at the moment, but it fueled me to return home all the sooner. I'd had enough of the Underworld.

Chapter 19

Thanks to my enhanced artifact, courtesy of
Hermes, I easily found my way back through the gate.
Hermes had said the boost he'd given it would allow
me to pass through and back again, so I assumed it
had now lost whatever power he'd instilled into it. But
just as when he'd powered it up, if the magic had
faded, I couldn't tell. Godly magic must work on a
spectrum that my mortal wizard's senses could not
detect.

I took a moment to orient myself with my
surroundings, trying to remember the best path to
return to my entry point. The Underworld's very
nature played hell not only on my sense of time, but
my sense of direction as well, so it took me a few
minutes of focused thought before I remembered how
I'd gotten here.

That's when I heard it. Chaos. Pure, unadulterated chaos. There was an enraged leonine roar and the sound of men shouting. Then, the unmistakable sound of gunfire echoed across the expanse.

Anger welled up inside me. I knew I'd let those Aegis agents off too easily. Staff in hand, I began sprinting towards the noise for all I was worth. My body protested the decision. Aches and pains accrued from my altercation with Cerberus reared their ugly heads, but I ignored it all. I had to stop this before something terrible happened.

The roars and snarls continued, but they were becoming weaker and more pained. I gritted my teeth. I had to run faster, but I was already moving as fast as my legs would carry me. I began running up a high slope, the sounds of fighting were coming from the other side. If I could just—

There was one long, pained roar that faded into a howl. Then I heard the crash as something big fell to the ground.

No. No it couldn't be.

I crested the slope to gaze upon the aftermath. Sure enough, there were a dozen Aegis agents surrounding a fallen hellhound. It was the same one as before, I was sure of it. But it hadn't been so lucky this time. Hellhounds were a force to be reckoned with, but even they would eventually fall to a coordinated assault. The poor creature was covered in blood. Judging by the several human corpses surrounding it, I knew that only some of it was its own. The beast had gone down fighting and had done its best to take as many of its assailants with it.

Anger welled up from deep inside me. The hellhound, while a mighty, violent beast, had been an innocent. It did not deserve to be hunted down and killed. And for what? So these foolish agents could study it? Try and turn its blood into some type of super soldier serum? It didn't matter. Without meaning to, I called up the Spring Flame that dwelled deep within me. All of my magic, especially my fire magic, was enhanced by the Spring Flame's mantle, but the Spring Flame itself was a whole other beast.

The fire that burned around my body shone brightly, basking the landscape as far as I could see in its warm, violet light. That was enough to get the Aegis agents' attention. They all turned to look up at me. I had no doubt they were as surprised and terrified as the hellhound had been when they had attacked it. I could hear their voices calling back and forth, no doubt trying to figure out what was going on and what they should do.

I swept my staff across my body and instantly sent several fireballs hurtling towards them. They had little time to react. Some ran for cover, others looked at the oncoming attack with dumbfounded expressions. But it didn't matter. The fireballs struck the ground in several spots so that they'd all be hit by my initial attack. The fireballs detonated on impact, releasing flame and kinetic force in all directions. Agents went flying through the air, letting out terrified screams. With what little sense I'd maintained amongst my rage, I'd planned my attack well. It wasn't meant to kill any of them. But it would burn, maim, and bruise them. Several agents crumpled to the ground, but others recovered quickly enough and trained their weapons on me.

"Fools," I thought.

Gunfire roared and a barrage of bullets sailed toward me. I hissed out a word and called up an invisible, kinetic barrier that stopped each of the rounds cold. Simply for added effect, I increased the heat of my fiery aura. As the bullets hit my shield, the heat from the flames melted them into glowing molten metal. Then I began walking toward them, all the while maintaining the shield and flames. I left a mess of the melted bullets wherever I walked, all the while inching closer and closer to the agents.

"Hold your fire!" A voice rang out over the noise.

The cacophony of bullets ceased, but I didn't let up on my shield or the fire that surrounded me. Agent Bardot approached me. Even though he was wearing the same protective gear as the rest of the agents, I recognized him from his gait alone.

"You just assaulted several of my men! I could have you arrested!" Bardot snarled.

I looked down on him with contempt. It was usually the least threatening men who felt the need to yell and snarl to intimidate their adversaries. I gave him my best cold steel stare and said nothing.

Bardot shifted nervously and cleared his throat. "If you leave now, I'll ensure nothing further comes from your interference."

I scoffed. "Your threats are hollow, Agent Bardot. And I warned you to leave before you did something astronomically stupid." I gestured towards the fallen Hellhound. "And now look at what happened. What'd you use, silver-point rounds?"

Silver was a common edge that men had over the supernatural. Most things from the supernatural had some degree of weakness to it.

Bardot looked over to the slain beast and then back to me. "How'd you know?"

"I'm a wizard," I said simply. "I know everything."

It wasn't true that I knew absolutely everything. But wizards had a reputation of knowing unknowable things, so I'd decided to lean into it here.

"I have half a mind to incinerate your entire squad, Agent Bardot," I said, my voice calm and level despite my gruesome threat. "It wouldn't be hard, you know. It'd take as much effort for me as a light jog."

"You don't scare me." Bardot spat, though I could hear his voice shake slightly.

"*Magnes*," I hissed. All of the agents' firearms flew from their grips and towards me. Though this time, the flames I'd called up instantly began superheating the weapons that I held in a floating cluster. It didn't take long for the guns to melt into an unrecognizable pile of slag. Satisfied, I let the heap fall to the ground, bubbling and oozing until it eventually cooled.

I looked back to Agent Bardot. "Leave. NOW." I used a voice amplification spell to make my voice much louder than I could've managed on my own. Bardot and his goons flinched away from the sound of my voice.

Bardot took a couple steps back. He glanced at his men, considering his options, and then back to me. "This isn't over, wizard."

"Yes. It is." I said. I let the flames surrounding me slowly die, as they were beginning to tax me more than I would've liked. "Leave. And this time, it's an order."

Without breaking eye contact with me, Bardot spoke to his men. "Let's move out!" His eyes narrowed. "We have what we came for."

I eyed him suspiciously but said nothing. I'd had enough trials and conflict for one day. I stood there, watching the agents retreat until I couldn't see them anymore. Then I turned my attention to the hellhound they'd unceremoniously killed.

Hellhounds were not traditionally beautiful creatures. They were ugly and brutal creatures, but given their environment, I couldn't blame them. Even so, I couldn't help but admire the beast. It was huge and powerful, but most importantly, it was intelligent. It had not wanted this fight. When I'd intervened the first time, the creature had understood I was rescuing it and it chose to run away.

But it didn't get the chance to run away this time. It had stood its ground, even when it was clear that it was fighting a losing battle. I cursed myself for letting the Aegis Institute agents off so easily the first time. Perhaps the hellhound would still be alive if I had been harsher with them.

A flicker of movement a ways behind the hellhound's corpse caught my attention. Dark shapes fled the scene. My eyes widened. They were hellhound pups, perhaps a quarter of the size of a full-grown hound. They ran up one of the many hills, and as they reached the top, the leader of the small pack looked back in my direction. It was too far away to tell, but I knew in my heart that it was taking one last look at its fallen mother. Then it went over the hill and was gone, along with its siblings.

I said a silent prayer, even though I didn't subscribe to any particular faith, for the beasts as they set out in this unforgiving realm without their mother's protection. I took one last look at the hellhound and then turned away to set off for home.

A very tiny howl pierced the silence.

I whirled around again, raising my staff on instinct. I eyed my surroundings, staying absolutely silent. Then the sound rang out again, the tiniest howl reached my ears once more. I strained my ears to follow the sound. It was coming from somewhere past the fallen hound. Again, the howl cried out. It was coming from the direction the other pups had run from.

I moved as quickly and as quietly as I could to where the sound came from. After climbing a small hill, I found a deep, cavernous opening in the side of a hill. Standing unsteadily just outside the cave's opening was the smallest hellhound I'd ever seen. It couldn't have weighed more than a couple of pounds and was about the same size as a large dog breed's puppy would be.

I knelt down, closer to the pup's level and set my staff down. The poor thing's eyes were barely open. Its mouth had not yet been malformed by misshapen teeth and its spinal flame hadn't yet sparked.

"You must be the runt of the litter," I said in a quiet, soothing tone.

The pup's attention focused on me and it let out a tiny growl that would've been ferocious coming from a much larger creature. It let out a snarling bark that shook its whole body. The pup stumbled once before righting itself.

"I'm not going to hurt you, little one," I shuffled slowly towards it.

The pup put on a brave show, but I could see its body shaking as nerves took over. I reached out slowly, offering my hand so the pup could smell me. The hellhound puppy lunged and it slashed me with its tiny teeth. I cursed, taking my hand back.

"You can't stay here, little one," I said. "Your family is gone and you will not survive on your own."

I did not know if the pup could understand my words, but I did my best to communicate my intentions to it. Hellhounds, like all dogs, understood body language and emotions well. I wanted the creature to trust me. An idea flashed through my mind. I unzipped my duffel bag and dug around inside. Amongst all the things I'd brought along to facilitate my trip here, I'd also packed some provisions. I pulled out an unopened bag of beef jerky and tore it open. Beef jerky was good to bring along when you weren't sure how long you were going to be gone. It lasted forever.

I tore off a small piece of the dried meat and tossed it towards the pup. It eyed me and then the food with a suspicious expression. Despite the hellhound being so young, it showed a certain level of intelligence. Then it took a couple hesitant steps towards the food. It only gave it one suspicious sniff before eagerly consuming the jerky.

I smiled and broke off a few more pieces and offered it to him. I'd determined the beast was a him, that is if basic biology applied to hellhounds. I kept feeding him until he'd emptied out my bag of jerky. Then the hellpup let out a big yawn, sneezed once, and waddled over to curl up at my feet. He was asleep before his head was down.

Adopting a hellhound wasn't exactly common practice, but my conscience wouldn't allow it. The pup was an orphan, just like my nephew. While it wasn't exactly the same situation, it tugged at my heart strings all the same. I scooped the hellhound up and did my best to make a comfortable spot for him inside of my duffel bag. Once I was sure he was safe and secure, I zipped the bag up most of the way, and decided it was time to finally leave this hell hole.

"So no trouble, then?" Braun asked me.

I handed him the leather pouch that held one of Hades' pomegranates. "No trouble at all. I sent the Aegis agents packing and procured what you asked me to."

"Well on behalf of myself and the rest of the High Elders, thank you, Bishop." Braun extended his hand.

I took it in a firm grip and we shook. Then I proceeded towards his office door. "You know Braun, next time, some backup would be appreciated."

"I'll keep it in mind."

I didn't see the old man's smile but could feel it as I walked out the door. Once I was safely back in Seattle, I peeked into my duffel bag just as the hellhound pup woke up. It yawned and looked up at me with intelligent eyes.

I had plans for the hellhound-to-be. He may be a runt, but the pup would still be a force to be reckoned with once he was full grown. He'd be a perfect guard dog, especially with what was coming for us in the future. It never hurts to have your own personal monster in your corner. And this hellhound had the makings of a monster, furiously loyal and incredibly powerful.

"Well, your looks will take some work, but I think you're going to be a valued member of the family...Scout."

Thank you for reading *Wizard Rising*, the first in the *Tales of Leight* series. These novellas will release occasionally and contain various short stories to complement the *Chronicles of Leight* and other future series set in the Leightverse.

Now that you're finished with *Wizard Rising*, I'd appreciate it if you could leave a review! Reviews are super critical for indie authors. It helps us grow and reach new readers.

Scan the QR code below to find all my links where you can keep up with updates on new books and projects!

Also consider signing up for my newsletter to receive a FREE exclusive ebook. *Gorgon's Blood* is a prequel story following Bishop Leight a hundred years before the main series.

If you enjoyed *Wizard Rising*, consider checking out other books by the author!

<u>Chronicles of Leight Series</u>

Fallen Son (Book 1)

Fang Wars (Book 2)

Gorgon's Blood (Book 0.1)

Dreambound Fae (Book 3) *Coming Soon!*

<u>Tales of Leight Novellas Series</u>

Wizard Rising (Book 1)

Reading Order

www.ingramcontent.com/pod-product-compliance
Lightning Source LLC
Chambersburg PA
CBHW010734100726
47899CB00009B/3042